"DON'T BURN MY MOTHER! "

This is a novel that runs like a movie ... a young American woman met a little boy in India who saw his mother burst into flames for dowry ...

❦

By

H. B. Thakur

INTERNATIONAL PUBLISHING HOUSE
445 West, 45th Street
New York, NY 10036

The story of this novel is a fiction, but not its background. The background, the burning of brides in India, is real. The problem was addressed by CBS Television Network in "60 Minutes" on November 11, 1984. According to CBS, about 500 brides are burned every year near Delhi alone.

"The Boston Globe" ran a befitting editorial on August 4, 1991. According to Boston Globe, the number is **11,259 in three years,** 1988, 1989 and 1990.

This book tries to analyze how India ... the seat of an ancient civilization ... could fall into the rut of moral decadence of such a magnitude.

   International Publishing House
   445 West 45th Street
   New York, NY 10036

Printed in the United States of America,
First Edition, $13.86 (U.S.A.)

November, 1991.

DEDICATED

to

Mrs. Naomi Rosenberg

for her support and sympathy
with the cause
about which
this book is written

ACKNOWLEDGEMENTS

My gratitude goes to my elder sisters who gave me a wonderful childhood, full of love and affection. Without them, I would have never written this book.

Mrs. Naomi Rosenberg, with her radiant support in all phases of the thought process, has championed the cause for which this book is written. I am specially grateful to her.

Dr. Herschel S. Shohan, Dr. Sita N. Kapadia and Mr. Robert Kinerk read the manuscript and made valuable suggestions. I also received very enouraging support from Ms Genevieve Moloney. Miss Riti Sachdeva designed the cover page of the book. I am indebted to all of them.

I thank CBS Television Network and "The Boston Globe" who tried their best to draw world attention to the problem. I hope they will keep up their efforts and help uproot the cause of the tragedy.

Finally, I request the reader to say a word in silent prayers for the souls of the innocent girls who were terminated at the prime of their lives in a holocaust that is still blazing unabated for the last three hundred years without any hope in sight.

"DON'T BURN MY MOTHER !"

[A Novel]

Have you ever seen a sunset over the Himalayan Mountains ? The breathtaking beauty of the snow-white peaks ... against the backdrop of the blue sky ... that gave the timeless music of the Ragas and inspired the ancient people to meditate on their existence ?

The irony, however, belongs to the present days. The sunset brought an ominous evening at the house of Mr. Tyagi at Moradabad, a crowded city some two hundred miles south of the Himalayas.

Moradabad is about one hundred miles east of India's capital, New Delhi.

Tyagi and his son, Shekhar, were not home at that time. Tyagi's daughter-in-law, Shekhar's wife of a few months, Kamla, was seated on a sofa in the living room, reading a magazine. She had a lot of red vermillion on the parting of her hair. Vermillion is considered very auspicious by a Hindu woman. It is the sign of marriage ... sign of good health of the husband. The newly married girls, being new to vermillion, overdo it ... they put a lot on their hair !

Shekhar's mother, Amba, a portly lady in her early fifties, had many reasons to hate her new daughter-in-law. Kamla's father was behind in the dowry installments, money needed to send Shekhar's sister, Rita, back to her husband's house. Unhappy words ricocheted between Kamla's parents and Shekhar's. Ultimately, Amba and Rita decided upon the "final" solution. They kept their plan absolutely secret from Shekhar, because, to their downright dismay, they knew that Shekhar was different from other Indian dowry bridegrooms: he loved his wife.

Noticing that Kamla was engrossed in reading the magazine, Amba signalled Rita to bring the bucket of kerosene oil, a petroleum product used as fuel in cooking stoves in India. Rita tiptoed to the back of the sofa with the bucket in her hands. Unaware of the imminent danger, Kamla was still engrossed in her magazine. She did not raise her head. She looked extremely beautiful in that angle, with a lot of red vermillion on the parting of her hair.

Amba was at the door of the living room getting ready with the matches. Rita suddenly unloaded the bucket of oil on Kamla. Taken by surprise, Kamla jumped out of the sofa and looked at Rita in utter disbelief. Instinctively, Kamla turned towards the door, where Amba was standing, holding a lighted match, the flame flickering eerily. At the next instant, Amba threw the lighted match. Kamla burst into flames.

Kamla came running to the door, pushed Amba onto the floor, ran past her to the streets, and kept on running. Her body was engulfed in flames, yet she kept on running, impelled by some super-human strength that people get just before death. Lots of noise. People in the street ran after her, shouting, gesticulating, with different

2

degrees of apprehension as to what happened.

" .... and that's how my wife died."

Shekhar was narrating the incident to his friends. It was a cookout party at a picnic spot in the Blue Hill mountain, overlooking the skyline of Boston in the U.S.A. It was sometime early in the decade of 1980's. People around were Nancy, Shekhar, Jim and Willy --- a group of 24-year olds. Their bags and T-shirts carried the insignia of the MIT and Harvard Universities. The soda cans, bags of chips, and a chicken rolling over a campfire indicated an impromptu afternoon picnic.

"But, that was murder ! And, nobody took any action ? ", Nancy asked in great surprise.

SHEKHAR: 500 brides are burned every year near Delhi alone.

This exploded like a shell.

"Five hundred ??", Nancy shouted in great surprise and distress. She worked many summers feeding the poor people in Mexico and South America as a Peace Corps volunteer. She could not digest this statistics silently.

JIM: I read about that.

3

WILLY: Didn't you see it on "60 minutes" ?

JIM: Yeah, ... hey, I saw that ! It was Harry Reasoner ... he went into how people there tried to hush it all up, and how Indian officials tried to stop the CBS investigation.

WILLY: It wasn't Harry Reasoner. It was Morley Safer.

JIM: You remember ?

WILLY: Of course I remember. It was Safer who clearly stated that the Government did not grant permission to film the story. CBS had to do it clandestinely ... those were his words ...

NANCY: Why ? You mean ... the Indian Government just lets this go on ?

SHEKHAR: That's why I don't want to go back to India. You guys will have to do it without me ....

Willy interrupted Shekhar. "But, you're the only one we know who has connections with Indira Gandhi".

SHEKHAR: *(Jeeringly)* My father has ... he claims he has. He is the famous Tyagi-ji, the Venerable Mr. Tyagi, of Moradabad ... everybody thinks he is the right hand man of Indira Gandhi. That's how he scares everybody. That's how he covered up everything and asked me to marry one more time ...

NANCY: One more dowry ?

SHEKHAR: And ... one more burning. *(A pause)* I ran away before that.

The subject became very personal. Willy tried to change it. "But, if you don't come with us ... how will we get all those Government permissions and visas in India and Nepal ... we need the connections, Shekhar ! You know this expedition is a kind of a secret ..."

Jim joined Willy in their attempt to convince Shekhar. "We cannot take any help from the mountain-eering clubs", Jim added.

NANCY: Why ? What's all this secret about ?

SHEKHAR: *(Surprised)* Why ? Neel didn't tell you ?

NANCY: *(Surprised)* Neel didn't tell me what ?

JIM: I thought you knew it. Neel did all the calculations.

NANCY: What's going on ?

WILLY: I'm sorry, Nancy ! If Neel didn't tell you, we shouldn't tell you either.

NANCY: *(Angrily)* How come Neel told you and didn't tell me ?

SHEKHAR: All right, Nancy, I'm going to tell you, but you must keep it a secret. Jim found it, but he didn't do the calculations. Neel completed all the calculations ...

NANCY: About what ?

SHEKHAR: The highest mountain in the world.

NANCY: That's Mount Everest, everybody knows that !

JIM: Not any more. We have found a peak that's even higher than Mount Everest. It is directly to the north of Kathmandu. We will be the first team to climb it.

Nancy realized the implications. "My God ! You'll hit the headlines !", she exclaimed.

"Until then, you'll have to keep the whole thing a secret", Willy cautioned.

Nancy was very offended. She thought she had a right to know it directly from her fiance, Neel. "How come Neel didn't tell me ?", she sounded as if she were asking herself.

JIM: Neel is a genius. I got those old records from the Geological Survey archives in London and he did all the calculations. I would have never completed those numbers without Neel.

NANCY: *(She was still very offended)* But why did you call me ? I'm in economics, I don't do any geodetic calculations !

WILLY: Because we want you to get a donation from your uncle.

JIM: We can't take help from any mountaineering club ...
you know why !

NANCY: I see.

WILLY: If you want I'll go with you to see your uncle.

NANCY: He is in the Bahamas. He has been very upset
since my mother died last month.

WILLY: You should tell him that his competition, the
Bradford family, is donating thirty thousand dollars !
Maybe you could call him.

JIM: And Shekhar could take charge of all government
formalities in India ...

SHEKHAR: As much as I can do it from here. But, I'll
never go to India, I told you why ...

NANCY: That's really tragic. Those girls are absolutely
innocent ! Neel did mention about the practice of dowry
in India, but he said his family is very progressive, does
not follow those old customs ...

Shekhar was surprised. He knew it was not true.
Neel must have lied to Nancy.

WILLY: *(To Shekhar)* Do you think Neel could have
helped us in India ? If you don't want to go ? To get all
those visas, inner-line permits, foreigner's permits, all
those Government permissions ?

SHEKHAR: You should have asked him before.

JIM: I'll ask him tomorrow.

SHEKHAR: Tomorrow ? He won't be here tomorrow !

JIM: What do you mean ?

SHEKHAR: You didn't know ? Neel is going to India tonight.

NANCY: *(Shocked)* What ?

SHEKHAR: *(To Nancy, with surprise)* Even you didn't know ?

NANCY: When did he tell you ?

SHEKHAR: He didn't tell me ! I came to know from his roommate, Prakash. Prakash was looking for some cheap airline tickets for Neel and called me. I thought you knew that.

NANCY: What airline is he taking ?

SHEKHAR: I don't know. The flight will be from New York. He is taking the PanAm Shuttle from Boston to New York. *(Looking at Nancy)* Why ? Do you want to ... I mean, try to ... stop him ?

NANCY: No. I don't want to stop him. I want to talk to him. He told me we would go to India together. His mother would fill up my lap with gold and silk; that's the ritual for taking in a daughter-in-law, he said. Then, she would put red vermillion on my hair. My own mother died last month, but I'd get a new mother, he said.

Jim was too much preoccupied with his own mountaineering plans to understand Nancy's frustration. "Well, if you meet him before he leaves, will you ask him if he could get those government formalities done for us ?", Jim asked Nancy.

WILLY: *(To Shekhar)* Do you think Neel's family has connections with Indira Gandhi ?

SHEKHAR: Neel's father also claims to be another right hand man of Indira Gandhi. Some kind of a party boss.

JIM: Well, I'll have to write to Neel. *(To Nancy)* Do you have his address in India ? Where are you going ?

Jim's concern was a little too late. Nancy had already stood up and left. They only saw her back. Her movements were so abrupt that Shekhar shouted in surprise, "Nancy, where are you going ?"

Nancy was walking very fast, almost running, downhill, towards the cars parked on the street. The skyline of Boston was tinted red by the evening sun. The glass tower of the John Hancock building was ablaze with red reflections. Shekhar was standing, gesticulating with his hands, "Nancy, please, don't go, wait !"

Willy assured Shekhar with the air of a man of

the world, "Don't worry, Shekhar, she'll be all right."

Jim was slow to understand this kind of things. "You guys don't think Neel dumped her, do you ?", he asked naively.

Willy, with his authentic managerial instincts, changed the subject. He asked Jim, "So, are you sure we are getting the check from the Bradford family Trust ?"

JIM: I am sure.

WILLY: That solves forty percent of the problem.

SHEKHAR: The remaining sixty percent ?

WILLY: Well, I have a few connections, I'll let you guys know in a day or two.

JIM: Oh, by the way, Shekhar, you'll have to get the permit for two hunting guns, not one. Do you think you can persuade the Consulate ?

SHEKHAR: I don't have the permit even for one hunting gun, Jim, and you need two ? The Indian Consulate is very touchy about guns.

JIM: Well, we're climbing a mountain which is not tried by any other team in the past. We must be ready for all kind of unknowns.

WILLY: *(Laughed)* What ? You'll need the guns to shoot the Yeti ?

JIM: *(Laughed)* I'll take a net for the Yeti. I need guns for snakes and tigers in the foot hills.

SHEKHAR: Well, I'll go now. I'm worried about Nancy. I want to go find her.

WILLY: That's none of your business, Shekhar ! Leave her alone. You'd better plan a trip to the New York office of the Consulate next week.

Nancy drove recklessly, and when she arrived at Neel's apartment building, Neel was packing his suitcase at his second floor apartment. His friend, Prakash, was standing at the window, keeping a watch on the street and hurrying Neel to pack up faster. When Prakash saw Nancy getting out of her car down at the street level, he ran into a panic. "Oh my God, Neel ! She is here !"

It was now Neel's turn to panic. "Did you say she's here ? What do you mean she's here !"

Neel came running to the window. "Oh my God, Prakash, what am I going to do now ?"

"Maybe she doesn't know ! Talk her into something else .... and then ...."

"No, n-no, I can't face her. What will happen if she already knows everything ?"

"All right. Put the suitcase under the bed and you hide in the closet. I'll tackle her."

They pushed the suitcase and all other things to be packed under the bed. Neel ran to hide in the closet.

12

The door-bell rang. Prakash opened the door. Nancy was at the door.

"Hi Nancy, how're you ?"

"Is Neel home ?"

"Neel ? Neel is not home ! He went out after lunch. He must be at the library."

"Which is the cheapest airline ticket to India, Prakash ?"

Prakash's face muscles had to work overtime to conceal his concern, "Why ? Do you want to go ?"

"Yeah. I'd go with Neel ... he told me. His mother would fill up my lap with gold and silk, that's the ritual to take a daughter-in-law ... he told me. Then she would put red vermillion on my hair ... the sign of a married woman ..."

"Nancy, you're an intelligent girl. Do you think you're doing the right thing ?"

"I'm doing what ?"

"If you marry Neel, there'll be a big problem in their family. They're strict vegetarian, I thought you knew that !"

"What about you, Prakash ? Are you a vegetarian, too !"

With extreme self-righteousness, Prakash deliberated, "Yes, of course."

"Why ? Why do you support vegetarianism, Prakash ?"

"Every living being is an image of God, you know. We cannot just burn a chicken like you do in a barbecue ...."

"But, if the father fails to pay the dowry, you burn the girl, don't you ?"

"Who told you that ?"

"500 brides are burnt for dowry every year near Delhi alone. Are their in-laws vegetarian or non-vegetarian ?"

"Shekhar must have told you. These are all exaggerated numbers."

What followed next was a standard vegetarian-non-vegetarian debate, mixed with another standard gambit: denial and scaling down of social evils.

"All right, Prakash, I'm sick and tired of arguing with you. If you meet Neel, tell him I'll wait for him at the airport", Nancy tried to conclude the conversation.

Prakash was caught off guard.
"Airport ? How do you know which airlines he's flying ?"

"Flying where, Prakash ? You said Neel has gone

14

to the library ! Tell him I'll wait at the PanAm terminal."

Nancy left.

Prakash knocked at the closet door. "Come out, Neel. We've a real problem here."

Before tackling the "real problem", the two friends blamed each other for the situation. Ultimately, Prakash drew the final line.

"Stop it, Neel. I didn't give her any clue. She must have heard from somebody. Or she is just bluffing. You don't know how dangerous these American girls can be."

"What will happen now ? I can't go to the PanAm terminal."

"The only way out is to drive to New York directly and catch the international flight from there", Prakash sounded like a military strategist.

Neel looked at the watch and interjected nervous- ly, "Yeah ! We still have six hours. But, there'll be traf- fic at New York City ..."

"We'll have to rush ...

But unfortunately, while Prakash and Neel were busy loading the car with Neel's luggage, Shekhar arrived there looking for Nancy.

"Where are you two rushing off to ?"

Prakash was very angry at Shekhar. "So, you're the guy ! You must have told Nancy ..."

SHEKHAR: Where are you going ? I thought your flight from Boston is at eight o' clock !

NEEL: It's all because of you ! Now we'll have to drive to New York to catch the international flight there.

PRAKASH: Why do you do this, Shekhar ? You should support your own country and your own countrymen ...

SHEKHAR: How much dowry is Neel's father going to get, Prakash ?

PRAKASH: What are you talking about ?

SHEKHAR: And how much commission is your father going to make ?

NEEL: This preposterous ! You're talking like that against your own countrymen ?

Prakash dragged Neel into the car.

"Come on Neel, it's late. We don't have time to talk to a traitor."

SHEKHAR: Very patriotic, hah !

PRAKASH: *(From the car)* We'll handle you later.

16

Neel and Prakash drove off. Shekhar looked at the receding car, jumped into his own car, and started to follow. He gave up the chase when he found out that they were definitely going to New York by road.

Shekhar was thinking of Nancy. When he arrived at the airport and found Nancy seated in the midst of so many unknown faces, waiting to see Neel who would never come there, he had a pang of guilt: he was responsible to introduce Neel to Nancy two years ago. Shekhar approached her and both of them went to a window, overlooking the planes taking off...

"There's no point waiting for him over here, Nancy !"

"I'll have to ask him before he leaves. He can't leave like this without telling me anything ..."

"Wha ... what do you want to ask him ?"

"When my mother died, he was the only one I was left with."

"I'll drive you home, Nancy, you're very upset, you mustn't drive today."

"You know, my grandfather and my uncle did not accept my mother because she married an outsider ... an ice-cream vendor ... outside their Sicilian community. All my life, I was raised alone by my mother. Even when she

17

became a widow, she refused to go to her father. I was then only a girl of eight, but I understood everything ..."

"But, when your mother passed away, everything changed, did you not tell me so ? That ... your uncle regrets everything ..."

"Yeah. He blames my late grandfather for everything and he is now trying to make up with me ... but it's too late ... after ... all those long years of deprivation ... a lonely life with a sick mother ...."

"Try to forget it, Nancy, and forgive ..."

"I must talk to Neel before he leaves ... "

"He ... he's not coming here, Nancy !"

She was surprised. "What do you mean ?"

"He's gone to New York by road."

"What ?"

In spite of all the indications, somehow, Nancy was not ready for the truth. She still hoped it was not so, that Neel would not do it.

Shekhar continued, "I followed them to the highway ... Neel and Prakash ... they're gone... "

"Prakash lied to me."

"You mustn't drive today. You come in my car.

I'll pick up your car later", Shekhar went on pleading.

"Prakash lied to me."

"Prakash must have made a lot of money by arranging the dowry for Neel."

"Dowry for Neel ? Neel told me his family does not ..."

"... take dowry, you said that before, but it's not true", Shekhar intervened. "A PhD from MIT ? His parents may easily get as much as six lakh rupees ..."

"How much is that ?"

"Six hundred thousand rupees."

"In dollars ?", Nancy asked.

"Thirty thousand dollars."

"And Prakash ?"

"His cut will be some three thousand ... maybe four thousand dollars ... ", Shekhar said cautiously.

Nancy pushed Shekhar to the side and ran towards the exit. Other passengers were surprised. Shekhar followed her in swift strides, "Wait, Nancy, wait ..."

Shekhar ran after Nancy. Nancy ran across the corridor, down the stairs, into the parking garage, got into her car, and drove off, tires screeching. Shekhar arrived there after Nancy's car was gone. He gave a look of despair towards Nancy's receding car, got into his car and followed swiftly. She did not stop at the toll-booth, broke the gate, broke the left headlight of her car, and drove off. The keeper of the toll-booth called the police.

Nancy drove recklessly through some residential neighborhood of Cambridge. Shekhar drove three blocks behind her, through a similar neighborhood, but on different streets. Shekhar stopped his car in front of Nancy's apartment. Nancy's car was parked at an erratic angle. The left head light was broken. There was no parking space. He drove to the end of the block, parked, came walking back to Nancy's car, looked at the headlight, walked towards the apartment.

When the door bell rang, Nancy was lying sprawled over the bed, face down, fingers into the hair. The door bell rang again. She heard Shekhar's voice, "Nancy, open the door."

Nancy did not raise her head when she replied, straining to keep her language straight, "Go away, you ... you Indian !"

Shekhar did not give up. He went on knocking at the door. "Nancy, please, open the door !"

Finally, Nancy opened the door, and asked very harshly, "What do you want ?"

"May I come in ?"

Nancy did not say anything. She went back and sat down on the bed. Shekhar came in, closed the door behind him, and sat down on a chair at a respectable distance from the bed.

"You shouldn't have driven. I had a hard time to convincing the police", Shekhar said.

"The police came ?"

"Of course the police came ! What else do you expect ? You don't pay your toll, smash the bar, break your headlight, drive off, and then expect nothing to be done about it ?"

"Are they coming over here now ?"

"No. I gave them my name and my license number. You're not in a position to face police at this time", Shekhar said.

Nancy was much relieved. "Oh, thank you. I don't know what I did ! I loved Neel so much ! How could he do this to me !" She got up and went to a window to conceal her tears.

"I am really sorry. I hope you'll have strength ... to get over this ... did you eat your supper ?"

"No", Nancy's reply was curt.

"Let me fix up something for you ... a sandwich, ... maybe ... what would you like ?"

"Forget supper. How much dowry is Neel going to get ? Thirty thousand dollars, right ? Didn't you say thirty thousand ?"

Shekhar tried his best to divert her anger. "Forget those things, Nancy ! Take a glass of milk, and try to sleep. I'll go now, and I'll talk to you tomorrow ...", Shekhar went to the refrigerator and took out a carton of milk.

"Didn't you say thirty thousand dollars ?", Nancy persisted, but without waiting for Shekhar's reply, she went to the telephone and started to dial.

"Whom are you calling ?"

"I'm calling my uncle."

"You don't have to call him now, it's past nine-thirty ..."

"My uncle doesn't sleep at nine-thirty when he is at a casino in Bahamas ...", Nancy had to cut Shekhar short and talk to the telephone, "Give me Agnitti, yeah, Vincent Agnitti... *(Pause)* ... he's not in his room ? Try him in the casino room downstairs, give him my name, Nancy ... Nancy Anderson"

At the Casino Room of Hotel Minerva in Nassau, Bahama Islands, an attendant brought a portable telephone to Mr. Agnitti who had to interrupt his game. His entire mood changed to warm affection when he heard Nancy's voice. "Nancy ! Nancy, baby, how are you ? Wait a minute, I can't hear you, hold on ..."

Agnitti moved to a comparatively quiet corner, followed by his bodyguards. He signalled the bodyguards to move away. He was evidently very happy to talk to Nancy.

At Nancy's end, it was a parade of emotional outbursts. "So, you do remember that your sister Susie is dead, but her daughter is still alive ...."

Agnitti was trying his best to defend himself. "No, I didn't say that, it was my father who ... *(Pause)* ... yes, I always wanted to ... *(Pause)* ... it was Susie's fault also, she should have ... *(Pause)* ... no, I'm not blaming a dead person, it was definitely my fault that I didn't ... *(Pause)* ... no, Nan, I love you Nan, you know that ... *(Pause)* ... of course, it's your money ... *(Pause)* ... you want to donate to whom ?"

Mr. Agnitti could not believe that Nancy was insisting on throwing away thirty thousand dollars to some mountaineering club. No doubt it was her money ... out of her inheritance after her mother died ... but Agnitti thought that Nancy did not know how to use money and that it was his duty to give her advice. But Nancy was adamant.

"Yes, you heard me right, Uncle Vinny", she went on arguing over the long distance telephone, "to a mountaineering club ... *(Pause)* ... no, I'm not throwing away the money, I'm throwing up ... *(Pause)* ... yes, throwing up, the money will climb uphill ... *(Pause)* they're climbing some thirty thousand feet in the Himalayan mountains in India .... *(Pause)* ... thirty thousand dollars ... *(Pause)* that's nothing. The Bradfords have donated double that amount, you always wanted to compete with the Wasps, you did, didn't you ?"

After some more argument with her Uncle Vinny, Nancy hung up the telephone and told Shekhar, "The money will be here tomorrow. Go and tell your friend Jimmy ... To his mountaineering team, I donate thirty thousand dollars, ... enough to buy his friend Neel, the math genius who recalculated their highest mountain peak in the world ..."

"You don't have to take matters so seriously, Nancy !"

"Do you know the meaning of the English word "serious" ?", Nancy quipped.

"Yes, I do. It is the brightest star in the sky."

"What ?"

Shekhar replied calmly, "The spelling is s-i-r-i-u-s, sirius, the most beautiful star in the sky, in the constellation Canis Major ... the world is beautiful, Nancy, you don't have to be upset over small matters ..."

"Small matters ? Neel dumped me, and you call it a small matter ? Just for some thirty grand, he went to marry somebody else, and you call it a small matter ? How could he ... how could he be so mean ? If he asked me I would have given him double that money. Money. Money. Money. What's the price of raw flesh in vege-

tarian India ? And human heart ? And honor ? And ...
and morality ? And kindness ? And love ?", she started to
cry.

Shekhar poured milk into a glass, kept the glass
on the bedside table and put the carton back in the
refrigerator. He could not stop an audible sigh. "You
have a right to be upset. Try to get some sleep now. I'll
talk to you tomorrow."

Shekhar walked to the door, but he did not go.
Nancy yelled at him, "Go away."

"I'll go as soon as you finish that glass of milk",
Shekhar replied calmly.

As if just to get rid of Shekhar, Nancy picked up
the glass and drank. When she finished the glass of milk,
Shekhar said softly,   "Good. And, good night."

"Thanks, Shekhar."

"See you tomorrow." Shekhar opened the door
and walked out.

After about a week, Shekhar went to "AGNITTI GUN & SPORT SHOP", accompanied by Willy and Jim. They came there to try hunting guns. Willy pestered the salesman to locate a gun at an unrealistic discount price. In that process, Shekhar spotted Nancy at the other end of the shop. Nancy had just entered the manager's cubicle, accompanied by two security men. Shekhar gave his car keys to Jim.

"You take the car, Jim. I've got to catch hold of Nancy."

JIM: What about her ?

SHEKHAR: I don't know what's going on. She hasn't returned my calls for a week. She ignored even the notes I left at her door.

WILLY: You worry too much. She is a little upset. Every girl is supposed to be upset when the boy-friend dumps her. She'll recover. She appears pretty tough to me.

SHEKHAR: It's all my fault. Do you remember, two

years ago, it was I who introduced her to Neel !

JIM: Don't worry, Shekhar. It is not your fault.

SHEKHAR: Let me go and find out what's going on. You guys take the car. I'll meet you at the dorm later.

Shekhar walked to the manager's cubicle. Inside, the manager was showing a silver colored pistol with a plastic see-thru handgrip and explaining to Nancy how to use it. There was an amber colored liquid in the plastic see-thru handgrip.

MANAGER: So, this will pass as a perfume dispenser. If you want to use it as a gun, just push this metal plate upwards and cover up the letter "P". It becomes a gun.

At this point, the manager, Mr. Gaggliano, saw Shekhar at the door. "Who are you ?"

Everybody looked at Shekhar who was standing at the door. The two security guards walked over and stood beside him, one on each side.

GAGGLIANO: *(To one of the security guards)* Did you leave the door open, Tony ?

Tony became very uncomfortable.

"I came to see Nancy", Shekhar said in his

28

characteristic unperturbed way.

"It's all right. He's a friend of mine", Nancy backed up.

"Well, Nancy, be careful", Mr. Gaggliano was visibly concerned, "your uncle will hold me responsible."

"Nothing will go wrong, Mr. Gaggliano," Nancy reassured, "we are very close friends."

Nancy put the pistol in her purse, exchanged greetings with Mr. Gaggliano, and left the store, followed by Shekhar. Shekhar kept on talking while walking, but Nancy did not reply. She walked faster, keeping one step ahead of Shekhar.

"I left so many messages in your answering machine but you didn't call back. Did you ever get the messages I left at your door ?", Shekhar's complaints sounded like a whining, which he continued as he rode in Nancy's car.

"I know you're upset. But, it is too much. You must see it rationally, talk to your other friends, ... life does not stop at one incident ... you should talk to your mother ... er ... I mean ... to your sister ..."

"I don't have a sister", Nancy interrupted.

Shekhar had to stop his chattering when he heard Nancy's voice. He tried to correct himself desperately, "Well, you definitely have a cousin, or somebody ...",

"Nobody. I don't have anybody."

Shekhar fell absolutely silent. He did not say another word till they reached Nancy's apartment.

"Does your uncle know that you're planning to go to India ?

"Yes. To collect data for my thesis, "Economic Strength of Rural India", under the guidance of Professor Kilgore of Harvard University, Department of Far East Studies ..."

"That's the official reason. Does your uncle know the real reason ?"

"If you remember Dr. Kilgore has been telling me to go to India since last one year. It was his idea to begin with. Neel and I both were supposed to go and collect data."

"Does Dr. Kilgore know what happened between Neel and you ...."

"He doesn't. He wants to see you, however."

"Me ? Why ?"

"Remember you gave him some writings of one Doctor Sharma of India, about a year ago ?"

"Yes. What about him ? They had been corresponding since then !"

"Not any more", Nancy remarked.

"Why ?"

"Ask him ! He wants to see you ! "

"Will you come ?"

"I better. Call him up. Here is his number."

Shekhar dialed the telephone.

When Nancy and Shekhar arrived at Dr. Kilgore's office that afternoon, they found him in a very serious mood.

"When I didn't get replies to my letters for about four months", Kilgore said, "I started to get worried. Doctor Sharma was very prompt in letter writing, no matter how busy he was with the publication of his news magazine."

SHEKHAR: News magazine ?

KILGORE: He started a news magazine after you left India. I don't think you saw it.

SHEKHAR: No, I didn't.

NANCY: *(To Dr. Kilgore)* Why did he stop writing to

you ?

KILGORE: I asked that question to the Indian Government. Yesterday I got the reply from them. Here it is.

      Kilgore fished out a letter from the pile of paper on the desk, and pushed it to Shekhar. Shekhar eyed it.

NANCY: What does it say ?

SHEKHAR: The Police charged Doctor Sharma for publishing unpatriotic articles in his news magazine, according to this Government letter.

KILGORE: They even said they found conclusive evidence that he had connections with the CIA.

NANCY: They found ... with the CIA ?

SHEKHAR: The letter says the Police went to Dr. Sharma's house to ask questions, and Dr. Sharma absconded. *(A pause)* Well, I know what that means.

NANCY: What ?

SHEKHAR: The Police must have raided his house without any search warrant. These things are very common there.

KILGORE: And did the Police find a connection with the CIA ?

SHEKHAR: Not necessarily. Police will plant whatever

they want to find ...

NANCY: That's quite a story.

KILGORE: Well, Nancy, when you go to India to collect data for your thesis, can you find out what happened to Doctor Sharma ? I want to correspond with this gentleman again. Of all the people I have contacted in India, I found him to be the most sincere. He dedicated his entire life to serve the people. First as a medical doctor. Treating poor patients without any fee. Then, as a journalist, he went out to write articles defending the victims of injustice. When the news papers refused to publish his articles, he started his own journal. He is something like a Mahatma Gandhi. I don't know why the Government should charge him with lack of patriotism.

SHEKHAR: Do you know what would have happened to Mahatma Gandhi if he were alive today ?

KILGORE: Are you also going to India, Shekhar ?

SHEKHAR: No, sir, I think I have explained to you, I'll never go back to India. For personal reasons ... I explained earlier...

KILGORE: Oh, yes, *(he remembers)* I know, I know ...

NANCY: *(To Kilgore, confidently)* Well, I'll find out what has happened, and write to you, or I'll try to telephone you.

KILGORE: Thank you very much, Nancy, but, please be

careful, I don't want you to get into any trouble ...

Nancy hoped against hope that Shekhar would ultimately accompany her to India. But Shekhar refused. He tried his best to talk Nancy out of her plan of going to India, particularly after he saw her gun. When he failed, he went to join his friends in the mountaineering team. They were exercising somewhere in the New Hampshire mountains.

Jim, Shekhar, Willy, and a younger new member of the team, Bob, were trying to negotiate a crest with ropes, pitons, carabiners, and other gadgets used in mountaineering. When they reached a resting place on the mountain top, they decided to take a break and pour some coffee out of a flask. The mugs of hot coffee turned out to be a most comforting thing at that place and time.

SHEKHAR: The Himalayan ranges ... you know ... will be many times harder than these New Hampshire mountains ....

JIM: We know that. We must practice in the Rockies.

BOB: Or, still better, in the Alps ...

Willy: Switzerland ? Forget it ! We don't have any money for that !

BOB: Come on, Willy, you can easily squeeze in a short trip to Alps with your flexible budget !

WILLY: No way. There is no money for Switzerland. Unless, of course, Shekhar can arrange another donation from Nancy.

SHEKHAR: *(Protesting)* I didn't arrange that ! She gave the money on her own !

WILLY: Can you make her give some "more" money on her "own" ?

JIM: After all, this is all Mr. Agnitti's money, isn't it ?

SHEKHAR: No. Nancy made the donation out of her inheritance.

WILLY: So, ... if it's her money ... she's free to donate more, isn't she ?

SHEKHAR: I don't know. Nancy is going to India in a day or two.

WILLY: Why ? *(Jokingly)* Is she going to kill Neel ?

SHEKHAR: Who knows !? Officially, she is going to India to collect data for her thesis and to contact a friend of her professor.

JIM: And, unofficially ?

WILLY: Well, that may be dangerous. Nancy might have had the luxury of being a Peace Corps volunteer ... working for the poor Mexicans ... but don't forget, her mother is from a mafia family.

SHEKHAR: *(Protesting)* But, she grew up without any contact with her maternal uncles !

WILLY: Doesn't matter ! A mafia is a mafia ! Do you have any idea how the mafia take their revenges ?

BOB: Who is this Mr. Agnitti ?

JIM: *(Laughed)* You never heard that name before ?

Everybody became silent for a while. Willy, with the budget on his conscience, broke the silence, "We should cut that Swiss exercise. Even if we get any extra funds, we should go to the Himalayas and do our exercises right over there. That'll be more cost effective."

BOB: That's a good idea. I've had some experience in the Alps. But the Himalayas ? That's different. I've read about them only in books.

JIM: Come on, let's finish this exercise. We'll talk about funds later.

Later in the week, when Shekhar arrived in Nancy's apartment, she was busy packing. She tried her best to avoid Shekhar, but that was not easy.

"You've not answered my question", Shekhar insisted.

"I answered that a million times. I'm going to India to collect data for my thesis and to meet ..."

" ... a friend of my professor", Shekhar continued on her behalf, "I know that answer".

"That's all."

"Are you going to take revenge ... I mean ... are you going to see Neel ?", Shekhar was pestering her.

"That's none of your business."

"Why are you taking that gun with you ?", Shekhar came directly to the point.

"Gun ? What gun ?"

"The one that you bought at Agnitti Gun Shop ?"

"That's not a gun ! That's a perfume dispenser", Nancy took it out from her purse and showed the transparent handle. "See, that's my favorite perfume", she pulled the trigger, and perfume sprayed out.

"That's very impressive", he took the gun from Nancy and tried. Perfume sprayed out.

"I told you so !"

She took the gun back from him and pulled the trigger. A shot, with a loud sound. The gun recoiled off her hand. Nancy was extremely puzzled.

"That's some perfume !", Shekhar picked up the gun from the floor and kept it on the table. Nancy was still puzzled. "I must have pulled the wrong lever."

"Does your uncle know that you're planning to shoot Neel ?"

"I'm not planning to shoot anybody. The gun is for self protection."

"Do you want me to believe that ?"

Nancy became angry. "Butt out, Shekhar ! This is none of your business."

Shekhar repeated in a very firm voice, "Are you

going to shoot Neel ?"

Nancy stared at Shekhar for a long time. At the same time, she put the gun back into her purse, without looking at the gun or the purse, and without taking her eyes off Shekhar.

NANCY: *(Very firmly)* No. I'm not going to shoot Neel. Let him have a long life.

She closed the zipper of the purse, without looking at the purse and without taking her gaze off Shekhar. She said the next sentence slowly, grinding each word separately ...

"I am going to kill his bride."

The 747 Jumbo Air India plane that Nancy boarded on her way to India had a painting of British Landing in India on the wall that partitioned one central aisle from the next. Nancy was very much puzzled. She wanted to ask the Air Hostess why the Government of India displayed the British Landing so proudly in their air planes. But, the Air Hostess was busy on the other aisle, behaving very rudely to an Indian passenger. When she came to Nancy's side, holding a tray of snacks very politely to Nancy and other white passengers, Nancy asked her what happened.

AIR HOSTESS: *(Almost confidentially)* He was trying to pay for the wine in Rupee currency, you know !

NANCY: *(Confused)* Rupee is the official currency in India, isn't ?

AIR HOSTESS: Yes.

NANCY: *(Surprised)* You don't accept that in the Air India ?

AIR HOSTESS: No.

NANCY: I thought the Air India planes are owned by the Government of India !

AIR HOSTESS: They are.

NANCY: Tell me, what's that painting .... one on the wall ?

AIR HOSTESS: *(Proudly)* That's a classic painting you know ! One of India's heritage ! We're very proud of our culture, you know !

NANCY: *(Confused)* But ... what's the painting about ?

AIR HOSTESS: Oh, it is showing the landing of British in the Madras port in the year 1640 ! More than 350 years now !

NANCY: And you call it your culture ?

AIR HOSTESS: Why not ?

NANCY: Well, I don't know. I thought you guys didn't want the British to rule over India and fought for independence.

It was night when the plane landed at New Delhi airport. Nancy went to stand in the line for Customs. She was very nervous whether her gun would pass through the customs. Some people broke the line and went ahead. Some people shouted: "Don't break the line. Stand in the queue."

Nancy observed every move of the person before her when he was checked. He was an Indian passenger. His box was opened and a collection of lipsticks, perfumes, etc., were found. The passenger separated some lipsticks and perfumes and told the customs official in a low voice .....

THE INDIAN PASSENGER: *(To Customs Official)* This one is for your wife, this one is for your daughter, this one is for your sister, sir ....

The Customs Official swept the stuff into a bag that was hanging below the table and said ...

CUSTOMS OFFICIAL: All right, all right, you may go ... who is next ?

Nancy came forward, opened her suitcase, dumped the load of lipsticks and perfumes on the table and started to say ...

NANCY: This one is for your wife, this one is for your daughter, this one is for your sister ...

The Customs Official was very pleased. "Thank you, thank you, Memsahib", he said. But then he saw the gun ! "What about this ? This looks like a gun !"

Nancy almost lost a heartbeat. But, she remained calm outside, and said quietly, "This is a used dispenser, a perfume dispenser."

She pulled the trigger, spraying the perfume. The Customs Official was very impressed. He smiled generously.

CUSTOMS OFFICIAL: Aha ! Let me see !

He took the gun and examined it with a lot of curiosity and appreciation. Nancy looked at it with great apprehension.

CUSTOMS OFFICIAL: *(Laughing)* It looks exactly like a gun, but it doesn't shoot bullets, it shoots something stronger than a bullet, ... reminiscence of a beautiful girl ... and the heart aches as if it is hit by a real bullet ...

He put the gun on his chest and pulled the trigger. Nancy felt as if the trigger was moving in extreme slow motion ! The Customs Official had a good spray of perfume on his shirt. He smiled, smelled the perfume in apparent ecstasy and returned the gun to Nancy who grabbed it with great eagerness.

However, a Customs Supervisor observed the delay from some distance and shouted, "Ramlal, why are you holding up the line !"

The Customs Official at the line became concerned. "Sorry Sir, it's all done Sir ... *(To Nancy, very politely)* you may go now Memsahib ... *(To the next passenger)* Who's next ?"

Nancy was surprised to get a royal treatment, particularly when the Supervisor came to escort her across the hall.

SUPERVISOR: I'm sorry if that official was giving you any trouble. Did he ask for any bribe ?

NANCY: No ! Why ?

SUPERVISOR: I have a lot of complaints about that man. If I can get one more evidence, I can suspend him from the job ...

NANCY: Why ? What has he done wrong ?

SUPERVISOR: I've practically cleaned up the department. He is one of the last guys who is still corrupt. Do you want to press any charge against him ?

NANCY: No !

SUPERVISOR: Well, that's your choice. And, he is lucky. By the way, where will you be going now ?

NANCY: I'll just take a taxi cab to my hotel.

SUPERVISOR: You mustn't ride a taxi alone at this time of the night. Is this your first visit to India ?

NANCY: Yes.

SUPERVISOR: That's why ! Which hotel ?

NANCY: *(Checking her note book)* Ashoka. That's the name !

SUPERVISOR: That's good ! There is an agent of Ashoka Hotel right here in the airport. He'll arrange transportation for you. You must not travel in a taxi alone, particularly at night.

He escorted her to a counter marked "Ashoka Hotel: Customer Service" and introduced to the man on the counter.

Back in the U.S.A., Jim, Willy, Bob and Shekhar met regularly to finalize their mountaineering plans. Maps, charts, photographs of mountain peaks, etc., piled up on the table in Jim's apartment.

WILLY: So ?

SHEKHAR: So I've changed my mind. I'll have to accompany you guys to India.

JIM: Bravo ! That's the best thing I've heard in a long time !

SHEKHAR: Not so fast, guys ! I'll go on the condition that you guys will help me to convince Nancy ...

WILLY: Hey Shekhar, hold it, forget about Nancy, we have a mountain to climb ...

SHEKHAR: And, I've a life to save. Maybe, two.

JIM: Maybe three, if you count Neel !

SHEKHAR: This isn't a joking matter, Jim. Yesterday, I got a call from Mr. Agnitti.

WILLY: What did he say ? Is he going to make one more donation ?

SHEKHAR: I didn't ask. He asked me about Harish, you know that MBA student in Yale ...

JIM: What about him ?

SHEKHAR: Agnitti wanted to make sure whether Harish is the son of the Chief of Police of New Delhi.

BOB: Oh my God, what are we getting into ? I thought we just had a simple plan to climb a mountain ....

WILLY: With no funds, on a mountain ten thousand miles from here, and some thirty thousand feet high ...

JIM: Don't tell the height to anybody.

BOB: I still don't understand how you figured out the height.

JIM: It's a top secret. The man who calculated the height of Mount Everest ...

BOB: He was Mr. Everest, wasn't he ?

JIM: No. Sir George Everest was the boss. The real calculator was one Mr. Radhanath Sikdar. Sikdar made some cryptic notes in Bengali which Neel deciphered.

BOB: I don't believe it ! How come everybody missed it for more than a hundred years ?

SHEKHAR: Well, the exact height of even Mount Everest was in controversy for a long time, anyway.

JIM: I followed Neel's translation and found another field book of trigonometrical survey in one of those London archives.

BOB: I still don't understand how people didn't see it before !

WILLY: Nobody figures out the tallest mountain by seeing it ! The next tallest mountain, K2, is only 777 feet less than Mount Everest, hardly four blocks. The next one, Kanchenjunga, is only 43 feet less than K2 ! You can't figure it out by eye judgement !

JIM: You have to go by the calculations. And there are so many factors that effect the field work ... snow level, gravity deviation, light refraction ...

SHEKHAR: The top piece of this peak of ours, Mount Shankara ....

BOB: That's the name of your secret peak ?

SHEKHAR: Yeah. The top piece of Mount Shankara, is a transparent ice rock, rising vertically into infinity ... that's what Sikdar wrote in his cryptic note.

BOB: Infinity !

JIM: Sikdar must have written that allegorically. We calculated the angular measurements. It is taller than Mount Everest by sixty-two feet.

BOB: I still think people would have seen the height when they went to climb Mount Everest.

WILLY: Its not like seeing World Trade Center towers from Empire State Building, Bobby ! Mount Shankara is one hundred miles west of Mount Everest, directly seventy miles north of Kathmandu, on the Tibetan side ....

JIM: We have a tough job.

SHEKHAR: When do we start ?

BOB: *(Excitedly)* Tomorrow !

WILLY: Not tomorrow !

BOB: We'll have to do lot of practice over there before the actual climb. And the month of May won't wait for you forever !

WILLY: I've yet to get those close circuit oxygen masks ...

JIM: Go get them, what are you waiting for ?

SHEKHAR: I'll get the visas endorsed. You finish up the rest.

Shekhar was now anxious to rush to India before Nancy did something really stupid, and that was exactly what she was trying to do. She called a taxi and asked the taxi driver whether he could find the address: Neel Bhatia, 32-B Nai Road, behind Chadni Chowk Market.

The taxi driver assured her that he could. He drove on all kinds of circuitous roads and Nancy got her first taste of a real car ride in India. She was not impressed by the pot-holes and broken curbs, she had a lot of these in Boston and New York and Philadelphia. What she enjoyed most was the way people blew their horns. Very soon she realized that there was some kind of a language in using the car horns, something like a Morse code ! By blowing the horns in different ways, with a little aid of gesticulation and shouting, the motorists in India could express all their feelings --- yell at each other, harshly demand a right of way, mildly lodge a complaint, patronize each other, even greet each other, or show off the grandeur of the ultimate status symbol ... the car ! People in the street talked in very loud voices --- they had to, to be heard over the din of car horns.

When the taxi stopped in front of the house, she asked the taxi driver to wait and went to knock at the door. The door was answered by Reena, a thin young girl in a sari. She had a frustrated look.

NANCY: Is it the house of Neel Bhatia ?

REENA: Yes.

NANCY: You must be his sister, Reena ?

REENA: *(Curious)* Yes ! How did you know my name ?

NANCY: Is Neel home ?

REENA: No. Please come inside !

They went inside, to the living room, where Tara, Neel's mother, a middle aged lady in a sari, joined them.

NANCY: Yes, Neel and I studied together. In fact, we have the same professor for our thesis. I've come to collect data for my thesis.

TARA: Collect data in India ?

NANCY: Yes. The subject is "Economic Strength of Rural India", the kind of things that your Mahatma Gandhi tried to promote.

TARA: *(Laughed)* Mahatma Gandhi ? You people still take him seriously ?

NANCY: Why ? Don't you ?

REENA: Nah ! He's kind of obsolete now-a-days !

TARA: Reena, go and make some tea.

NANCY: No, thank you, I won't need any tea at this time.

TARA: No, no ! You're a guest ! You must take something ! If you don't like tea, you may take laschi ...

NANCY: Laschi ! Is that something that you make with fish ?

REENA: *(Protesting vehemently, with a lot of self-righteous pride)* Fish ? No, no ! We are strict vegetarian. We don't touch fish and meat. Laschi is butter milk. You'll like it.

TARA: Call Sona and ask her to make the laschi with rose-water.

Reena shouted for Sona.

NANCY: Who is Sona ?

TARA: The maid servant. Reena, will you go and see ! I don't know where she has gone !

Reena went inside.

NANCY: So, how are the arrangements going on ?

TARA: Arrangements ?

NANCY: For Neel's wedding ?! In fact, I brought a gift for the bride.

Nancy opened her hand bag. The gun that looked like a perfume dispenser again popped up. Nancy picked up a perfume and gave it to Tara.

TARA: O, beautiful ! Thank you !! These foreign perfumes are so great ! Do you have some more ?

NANCY: Do you want one for your daughter ?

TARA: Do you have more ?

Tara stretched her neck to see the inside of Nancy's bag.

NANCY: I've plenty. I've one for you, one for your daughter ...

TARA: What's that ? A pistol ?

NANCY: No, it's a perfume dispenser ...

Nancy pulled the trigger, spraying some perfume.

TARA: That's really wonderful !   And the smell is so good.

Reena came to the door and called her mother by

signal. Tara excused herself and went to the kitchen.

TARA: *(To Reena)* What ?

REENA: *(Very angrily, but in a cautious, hushed voice)* Sona is not home. She is getting to be too much. You must give her a beating today.

TARA: *(Very angrily, but in hushed voice)* Yes. I'll give her a hell when she comes back. Can you make it ?

REENA: Which glass shall I use ?

TARA: Use the one from that shelf. Keep it separately, don't mix it up with our home glasses. I'll have to get it boiled in soap water after that *(in a very hushed voice)* beef-eating American girl drinks from it.

REENA: Let's wait till Sona comes.

TARA: No, no, don't delay. That American girl has a lot of foreign perfumes and lipsticks.

Tara came back and joined Nancy in the living room.

NANCY: So, you have got all the gold and silk you need for your future daughter-in-law ?

TARA: You know everything about Indian wedding !

NANCY: Well, this is all part of my thesis. Perhaps you can help me with the details !

TARA: Wait a minute, let me bring the box.

Tara went inside by another door and brought a suitcase.

NANCY: Great, you got all organized !

TARA: Not all ! We're still waiting for foreign lipsticks and perfumes.

Tara opened the suitcase and showed the gold and silk collected for the future daughter-in-law. Nancy had a strange feeling at the bottom of her heart ... she felt a strange, vague attraction to all these gold and silk ... a feeling that didn't make sense any more ...

NANCY: And this one is a necklace ?

TARA: No. That goes on the hair, on the parting of the hair, you know !

NANCY: And the silk ? Are they all tailored ?

TARA: These are saris from Banaras. We have to get some work done on the borders.

Reena entered with a glass of buttermilk on a tray. Nancy took the glass.

NANCY: Won't you join me ?

TARA: Not now. This one is for you.

NANCY: *(Drank buttermilk)* Ah, this is good !

REENA: Thank you.

NANCY: *(Pointing to gold and silk, and suppressing her own feelings)* This is really beautiful ! Your daughter-in-law will look beautiful in those silk and gold ! Do you think I could come and see the ceremony ?

REENA: That'll be in two weeks. All our relatives will be coming by that time.

NANCY: Two weeks ? I'll move to the Hostel of International Students by that time. What's the bride's name ? What's her address ?

REENA: Her name is Laxmi ... Laxmi Dwivedi. The ritual will take place in the house of the bride, see, the address and time and date are all given here.

Reena gave a wedding invitation to Nancy.

NANCY: Maybe I'll get a chance to see Neel that day.

TARA: No. Neel cannot go to the bride's house that day.

NANCY: *(Surprised)* How come ?

REENA: That's the bride's ritual, the bridegroom can't see her that day ! It's called Godbhari, meaning "Fill up the lap of the Bride".

NANCY: That's beautiful. Very poetic. And, that's not the wedding, right ?

TARA: No. The wedding will be some time later. You must come to the wedding. I'll tell Neel when he comes home.

NANCY: That's so nice of you to invite me. So, Reena, what do you want for your Godbhari ?

Reena got a shock.

REENA: My Godbhari ?

NANCY: Yes !

Reena started weeping, covered her face with her hands, got up and ran inside.

NANCY: *(Very surprised)* What ? What happened ?

TARA: That's not your fault. I should have told you earlier.

NANCY: Why ? What's the matter ?

TARA: There is no more Godbhari for Reena.

NANCY: Why ?

TARA: She is already married. Her in-laws rejected her.

NANCY: Rejected her ? What about her husband ?

TARA: Husband ?? The husband doesn't have any say in these family matters ! The mother-in-law, the father-in-law, they sent her back.

NANCY: Why ?

TARA: They have given us a one year grace period. That'll be over in three months.

NANCY: Grace period for what ?

TARA: If we can't come up with the balance of the dowry money, their son will marry another girl.

NANCY: What're you going to do about that ?

TARA: Reena's father is getting in touch with Phulraj Mathur ...

NANCY: Who's he ?

TARA: He's the private secretary of the Prime Minister, you know ! He is a very powerful man. If he wishes, he can ask the other party to give us some extra time.

Back in the taxi, Nancy told the taxi driver to drive to --- she read Neel's bride's address from the wedding invitation --- "53-A, Near Mango Tree, on Kangra Street, behind Sadar Bazar Road". The taxi sped off.

In Neel's house, Reena was recovering from her emotional shock. She was lying on sofa, with her face down. Her mother, Tara, was trying to console her.

TARA: Get up Reena, it was not her fault, she didn't know anything about your condition. When I told her, she was so sympathetic, see, she gave so many things to you.

Reena looked at the collection of lipsticks and perfumes on the center table.

TARA: She said she would bring more things for you later.

At this time Sona sneaked in and tried to take the tray without being seen by Tara and Reena. She was a fourteen year old servant, with a thin but sweet face, virtually in rags. She had a guilty look on her face and a little bundle in her hand. Tara saw her.

TARA: Where did you go, Sona ?

Sona froze on her track in fear.

SONA: I went to learn the doll-making at Kornel Uncle's house, Memsahib !

She raised her little bundle, revealing a six inch doll of a girl with an innocent face in a gorgeous costume.

Reena sat up. Her face grimaced in frustration and hatred.

REENA: Aha ! Another doll making session ! She goes to become an artist and I do her job !

SONA: I'm sorry, Reena Didi, but Memsahib told me I could go in my off hours.

Sona said "Reena Didi" very softly, meaning "Sister Reena", with respect and fear, hoping to please her, but nothing worked. Reena flared up.

REENA: You despicable vagabond, you dare speak back to me !

Reena charged towards Sona. Sona ran to the kitchen, where Reena caught up with her and started hitting. Sona tried to extricate herself. In the process, Sona pushed Reena. Reena fell on the slippery kitchen floor, and wailed ...

REENA: She hit me, she hit me ...

Tara ran to the kitchen. She flared up when she saw Reena on the floor.

TARA: *(To Sona)* You hit my daughter ? You hit my daughter ?

SONA: No, Memsahib, no, I didn't ....

Sona's entreaties were of no avail. Tara picked up a log meant for the wood stove. She gave a full swing to her hand and hit Sona with the log with all her strength. Sona shouted and fell on the floor, blood all over her face.

Sona's cries were heard by the neighbors. The next door neighbor, Mr. Saxena, an elderly man, apparently an ex-military personnel as it appeared from his well built physique, came out running to her aid.

When Mr. Saxena arrived at their kitchen, both Tara and Reena were beating Sona mercilessly. Sona was now half conscious. Saxena intervened. With strong muscular hands, he pushed Reena and Tara back, and made himself a shield between Sona and her assailants.

SAXENA: Oh my God, she is almost unconscious ! How could you beat a child like that ?

REENA: You don't have any right to be here. This is our house.

TARA: Do you know, I could call the Police for your trespassing.

SAXENA: Please call the Police. The poor girl will have some protection from the Police, I'm sure.

Saxena wiped blood from Sona's face. He lifted her unconscious body.

SAXENA: I'm taking her to my home for treatment. You call the Police. I'll talk to them.

He carried Sona to his house. Sona's little doll was on the floor, smeared with blood.

TARA: This man lost his military job for this kind of things. Now he will go to jail.

REENA: Do you want me to call the Police ?

TARA: *(Cautiously)* No, no, … not now. Let your father come. We will tell this to Phulraj Mathur.

In his house next door, Saxena and his wife were washing the wounds of Sona, giving her a bandage around the face, making her drink some water and a hot soup, making her lie down comfortably on a bed. Sona threw her arms around the neck of Mrs. Saxena and cried.

In the mean time, Nancy arrived at the house of Neel's bride, Laxmi. Her knock was answered by an old male servant in a dirty Dhoti and a ragged turban.

NANCY: Is this the house of Laxmi Dwedi ?

The man did not understand. He saluted feebly, signed her to wait and went inside. Chhaya, Laxmi's mother, an elderly woman in a sari, came out to receive Nancy.

NANCY: Is it the house of *(read from the invitation)* Laxmi Dwivedi ?

CHHAYA: *(Very hospitable)* Yes, yes, please come in !

They settled down in the living room.

NANCY: I am a friend of your future son-in-law, Neel. We studied in the same college ...

CHHAYA: *(Excited)* Oh ! You are also from MIT ?

NANCY: Yes. I've come to India to collect data for my thesis on Indian economy. Do you think I could see Laxmi ?

CHHAYA: Oh, yes, of course, but she's not home now, she has gone to her college.

NANCY: Oh ! Which college ?

CHHAYA: She goes to Miranda Girls' College, they're very busy now, organizing some dance groups and music for the youth festival ...

NANCY: So, will it be difficult to see her ?

CHHAYA: Oh no, no, you could in fact go to her college and meet all the girls ... it's a girls' college, you'll like it ...

Nancy got up. Chhaya did not have the slightest idea that Nancy was carrying a loaded gun, bullets meant for her daughter. With the customary Indian style of hospitality, Chhaya started to force Nancy to eat something before she could leave her home !

CHHAYA: Oh, no, no, no, you can't go like that, you're a guest, you must take something, would you like to have a cup of tea ?

NANCY: *(Politely)* Thank you very much, but I've to go, some other time .....

Chhaya opened her mouth to say something, but Nancy intervened ...

NANCY: No, not even laschi ....

Nancy laughed. Chhaya was surprised, but she also joined in the laugh ...

CHHAYA: So you know everything ... how long you have been here ?

NANCY: Only two days. I'm still at the hotel. I'll be moving to the hostel next Tuesday. I wanted to come and see the ritual where your daughter will get all the gold and silk and blessings and acceptance ...

Nancy was not laughing during her ride to Miranda Girls' College. "How long will it take to Miranda College ?", she asked the taxi driver, impatiently.

TAXI DRIVER: Just a few more minutes, Memsahib !

NANCY: Your meter is showing more than three hundred.

TAXI DRIVER: That's three hundred rupees, Memsahib.

NANCY: How much will that be in American dollars ?

TAXI DRIVER: I don't know. If you go to the Bank, they give you fifteen rupees for a dollar. But, if you pay me in cash dollar bills, my boss will agree to twenty rupees for a dollar. But, you mustn't tell the police.

NANCY: What about the shops ? The fashion shops that sell silk sari and gold jewelry ...

TAXI DRIVER: They can't take cash dollars openly. But, I know a few shops, they'll make some deal, and they sell beautiful Banarasi sari ... do you want to buy ?

NANCY: Yes. I'll have to buy one beautiful Banarasi silk sari to give to myself. There's no one else to buy it for me. There's no one else to fill up my lap with gold and silk and blessing and acceptance ....

The Taxi Driver failed to understand.

TAXI DRIVER: *(Surprised)* Memsahib ?

Nancy grasped the gun in her handbag and asked impatiently, "How far to Miranda College ?"

Arriving at Miranda College, Nancy asked the taxi driver to wait and went straight inside. In the hallway, she met a group of twenty-year-old college girls, named Gita, Mina, Neeta, Maya, Tina, etc., wearing jean pants, shirts and salwar-kameez. They flocked enthusiastically around Nancy.

GITA: You're also from MIT ?

NANCY: Yes.

MINA: O my God, that's exciting !

NANCY: Which one of you is Laxmi ?

NEETA: Laxmi ? Laxmi is the luckiest girl ! She got a groom from MIT !

NANCY: Where is she ?

MAYA: We've just finished our rehearsal. She has gone to change.

NANCY: What's this all about ?

TINA: We're having a cultural show next Sunday.

GITA: There'll be a lot of folk dances from all parts of India.

NANCY: You're bringing troupes ?

MINA: No. We have students from all parts of India right here in New Delhi.

NEETA: Our college will contribute one item.

NANCY: What's that ?

MAYA: "Break the Chain" -- that'll be a group song offered to Mother India ...

NANCY: What's the meaning ?

TINA: Laxmi will play the role of Mother India in chains, and we'll have a revolution to free her from the British Rule ... it's something historical, you know !

NANCY: I see.

GITA: Laxmi had to try her sari in the dress rehearsal today ...

NANCY: You girls don't wear sari ?

MINA: Only occasionally. None of us are good at that !

NANCY: How come ?

NEETA: The Sari is for old ladies, you know !

All laughed.

MAYA: Oh, there she comes !

Maya was pointing to left where Laxmi was coming down the hallway. She was carrying a small bag of costumes. She was very beautiful. The girls ran towards her and pulled her to Nancy.

GIRLS: Laxmi, Laxmi, see who's here ! *(meaning Nancy.)*

MAYA: She is a friend of your groom in MIT !

NANCY: You are Laxmi ?

LAXMI: *(Smiled)* Yes !

NANCY: I've got some gifts for your wedding.

LAXMI: *(Very sweetly)* Oh, thank you.

NANCY: I had to come to India to collect data for my research work, so all our friends had me bring their gifts to you. Your groom, Neel, is very popular in our class, did he tell you ?

LAXMI: No !

GITA: She has not even talked with Neel, she never got a chance !

NANCY: *(Surprised)* What do you mean ?

MINA: Don't worry, Gita, they'll have plenty of time to talk later. *(Everyone laughed.)*

Nancy was surprised. She asked Laxmi, "You did'nt even get a chance to talk to him ?"

Laxmi shook her head and smiled. Nancy was very surprised.

NANCY: So ... you didn't know him from before, did you ?

Laxmi shook her head and smiled. Nancy did not understand how the arranged marriages worked in India, but she did understand that this girl was absolutely innocent.

NEETA: She never fooled around with any boy before ...

MAYA: That's why God gave her an MIT boy for husband.

TINA: Not God ! Her father got that MIT boy !

MAYA: *(Protesting)* Only because of God, her father could get such an expensive boy.

NANCY: Expensive ?

GITA: Of course ! Do you know the price of an MIT boy in the dowry market ?

NANCY: Dowry market ? That sounds odd ! You girls

don't mind it ?

MINA: *(Surprised)* Why should we mind ?

NEETA: Our parents earn and save a lot of money to buy our grooms.

MAYA: We know it's hard on poor people. But poor people get a poor groom, rich people get a rich groom, that's how it works.

NANCY: I'm surprised. That's how you accept it ?

TINA: I know what you mean ! I've seen it in the English movies. The system is different in your country.

NANCY: *(As if she is talking to herself)* Market ! That sounds like a cattle market in my country !

While Nancy was having trouble adjusting to India, her friends in Boston were getting ready to take off. At Boston's Logan Airport, Shekhar, Bob and Jim were busy checking their luggage.

JIM: Where's Willy ?

SHEKHAR: He went to pick up a last minute donation.

BOB: I wanted to check with him about those close-circuit oxygen masks.

JIM: What about them ?

BOB: We should try each one of them before leaving.

SHEKHAR: There's no time for that now !

About this time, Willy made his last minute arrival.

JIM: There he is !

BOB: Hey Willy, did you check the oxygen masks the

way I showed you ?

WILLY: Yes, I did. Did you think I'd pay for them without checking all of them ?

SHEKHAR: Where you've been so long ?

WILLY: *(Smiling)* Surprise !

Willy took out a check to show them.

JIM: What's that ?

WILLY: A last minute donation ! See, fifteen thousand dollars !

Shekhar took the check, read it, became very grave and passed it over to Jim.

SHEKHAR: Why did you take a check from the Alpine Club ? I thought you were going to Ford Foundation !

WILLY: *(Defensively)* I'll go anywhere to make up our deficit.

JIM: But, you were not supposed to take a check from the Alpine Club ! What'll happen if they tell the Royal Geographic Society ?

WILLY: The Alpine Club knows nothing about our secret peak.

BOB: Are you sure ?

WILLY: Absolutely ! *(Impatiently)* Damn it, you can't go to a foreign country with insufficient funds !

JIM: If the Royal Geographic Society gets the jump on us ....

SHEKHAR: Do you know, they didn't even want the name of Tenzing Norgay because he wasn't British !

BOB: *(Laughed)* And we're worse ! We're American !

After a few days, there was a knock at Nancy's door and she was surprised to hear Shekhar's voice in response to her "Who's that ?"

"Shekhar. Open the door, Nancy !"

Nancy opened the door.

"Glad to see you. I thought you'd never come to India."

"I had to come because of you", Shekhar replied.

"What happened to your mountaineering team ?"

"They're all here. They're in a hotel, Hotel Meredith."

Nancy smiled. She was genuinely happy to see Shekhar. "How did you find me ?"

Shekhar laughed. "I had to do a little detective work."

"Did you have any trouble with the customs officials ?"

"Not much. What about you ? Did they see your perfume dispenser ?"

"That's a long story !"

Very cautiously, Shekhar opened the touchy subject, "Have you met Neel ?"

"No. But, I met his bride."

Shekhar was really alarmed. "Oh my God, what happened ?"

"Nothing. She's innocent."

Shekhar was obviously relieved. "I'm glad you liked her."

"I didn't say I liked her."

Assured that nothing had gone wrong so far, Shekhar went into another subject, "Did you see Doctor Sharma ?"

NANCY: No. I've just got an address, supposed to be his. I've not yet tried.

SHEKHAR: Listen, your uncle Mr. Agnitti called. I've some messages for you.

NANCY: Oh !?

76

Shekhar sat down and pulled out a note-book.

SHEKHAR: Number one, if you ever ... ever ... get into trouble with Police over here, call this gentleman ...

Shekhar tore a page from the notebook and gave it to Nancy. Nancy read the name ...

NANCY: Roshan Dixit. Who is he ?

SHEKHAR: He is the Police Chief of the Delhi area. Memorize the name. That's your uncle's instruction.

NANCY: Why does he think I may have problem with Police here ? You must have told him.

SHEKHAR: No. I didn't tell him anything. But, he knows you've got a gun.

NANCY: How does --- *(she consulted the note again)* Mr. Roshan Dixit ----- come into the picture ?

SHEKHAR: I don't know. But, Mr. Agnitti asked me if Harish was his son.

NANCY: Who is Harish ?

SHEKHAR: You don't know him. Harish Dixit. He is an MBA student at Yale. And, he is Roshan's son.

NANCY: Oh my God !

Nancy suddenly became quiet. She knew these

were not joking matters when her maternal uncle was involved.

SHEKHAR: And the second message is ...

NANCY: What ?

SHEKHAR: Call your uncle. Immediately. Right now. That's the second instruction.

NANCY: Do you know what time it is in the United States at this hour ?

SHEKHAR: Yes, I know. It's three in the morning. But that's his instruction. He gave this telephone number.

Shekhar tore another page and gave it to Nancy.

NANCY: Anything else ?

SHEKHAR: Yes. Your uncle's bodyguard Freddie came over and gave me this. Five thousand dollars. Call him if you need more.

Shekhar took out an envelope and gave to Nancy.

NANCY: How did you bring all these cash dollar bills through the customs ?

SHEKHAR: *(Jokingly)* I'm turning into a mafia boss myself.

NANCY: What's your plan ? Will you come with me to see Doctor Sharma ?

SHEKHAR: Forget about Doctor Sharma. Your uncle wants you to go back home immediately.

NANCY: But I've some unfinished work here.

SHEKHAR: Like taking your revenge. Forget about it, Nancy. Life is too valuable to be spent on revenge.

Nancy was quiet for a while.

SHEKHAR: You said you saw Neel's bride. What is she like ?

NANCY: Very innocent.

SHEKHAR: That's better. Now you should go home.

NANCY: I must see Doctor Sharma. Maybe he can answer some of my questions.

SHEKHAR: Like what ?

NANCY: Why they call me Memsahib ? Everybody calls me Memsahib and talks very respectfully to me. Why ?

SHEKHAR: Because you're white. The British ruled India for two hundred years. Indians respect all white people subconsciously.

NANCY: And Memsahib ?

SHEKHAR: The first half, Mem, is the short of Madam, another legacy of two hundred years of British rule. The second half, Sahib, is from seven hundred years of Islamic rule. A nation changes its genes in eight hundred years of foreign domination, like the ancient Britons under Roman rule.

NANCY: And, people here seem blind to a lot of things.

SHEKHAR: Who ? Which people ?

NANCY: The girls in Miranda College. They don't mind the dowry system.

SHEKHAR: Miranda College ? I've a cousin studying there.

NANCY: They invited me to their cultural show. Would you like to go with me ?

SHEKHAR: To the cultural show ?

NANCY: Yes. It should be fun !

The auditorium was packed in Miranda College. Nancy and Shekhar were lucky enough to get seats in the front row. The curtain was closed. People were still coming. If they did not find a seat, they would stand everywhere, blocking the aisles, in a very disorderly fashion. The function started one hour late. A girl dressed in a sari was making some announcements in a microphone in front of the curtain.

ANNOUNCER: We are very sorry for being late in starting our function tonight. As you must have read in the brochure, this is an evening of our heritage in which we will try to show India and the history of our struggle to free our motherland from the British rule. People of our generation did not experience the history of the previous generation that went through all the sacrifices during the struggle for independence .....

Nancy asked Shekhar, "When did India get her freedom ?"

"In 1947. You must have seen that in the movie, "Gandhi" !"

"I did. But, I don't remember much."

"You should see it again, if you want to understand India", Shekhar said.

In another part of the audience, Reena and Tara were seated with a vacant seat near them. One man came to take that seat. Reena told him that it was someone's seat. Tara kept her handbag to occupy that seat. Reena told Tara in a hushed voice...

REENA: Where is Neel ?

TARA: I don't know. He must have got tied up with your father and Phulraj Mathur.

In the mean time, the Announcer resumed her announcements.

ANNOUNCER: As the Nobel Laureate poet Rabindra Nath Tagore said, "India is not merely a piece of earth. It is a conscious soul." That consciousness is manifested through the people of India. We will try to show the People of India through their songs and music and folk dances. We will start from the four corners of India ... Nagaland, Assam on the East, Kerala and Marathas on the South, Kashmir and Punjab and Gujarat on the West and people of the Himalayas on the North. This will be followed by all the people of the mainland ... from Bihar to Gujrat, from Bengal to Rajasthan ...

While the announcement was going on, Nancy could not suppress her curiosity and asked Shekhar, "How big is India ?"

"Land area or population ? Which one do you want ?"

At this time, Neel arrived. He was about to enter the hall from the front, but he froze when he saw Nancy talking to Shekhar in the front row. In panic, he started to back. Shekhar or Nancy did not see him. Nancy continued her question to Shekhar ...

NANCY: Both.

SHEKHAR: Land is one point three million square miles, one-third of the United States. In population, some seven hundred million people, three times that of the U.S.A. !

NANCY: Wow !

By this time, Neel had backed up enough to reach the door. Now he turned around and started to run away in the corridor, while the Announcer was making the announcements in the stage ...

ANNOUNCER: And here we have a folk dance from Nagaland ...

The curtain opened. There was a huge map of India at the rear of the stage. A light was blinking on the eastern border of India. A dancing troupe entered from the left and displayed a very powerful folk dance in extremely colorful costumes of the Angami Nagas.

As the dance gained tempo, it appeared as if the background changed into the green hills of Nagaland with

Naga women transplanting paddy in the terrace cultivation on the hillside which was accentuated by a blue sky with white clouds.

The Announcer now announced: "Then we go to the golden rice fields of Assam and join them in their Bihu dance ..."

The map of India was seen again with a light blinking in an eastern region, Assam. The map was covered by a screen painted with a view of Assam plains, with the golden paddy cultivation on the banks of a wide river, the Brahmaputra, and an intense blue sky with floating white clouds. A group of dancers entered from the left, dancing to the tune of Bihu music.

Announcer's Voice Over: Now we take you to the Southern tip of India and show you the Temple Dances of Madurai.

The map of India was shown again, a light blinking on the Southern tip of India. A group of dancers entered from the left, giving the classical temple dances of Bharat Nrityam with highly developed music and rhythm and extremely complicated footwork to match.

Nancy was very impressed. "It is beautiful", she said.

"And complicated", Shekhar quipped very promptly.

NANCY: I'll like to go to Assam and Nagaland.

SHEKHAR: You can't go there.

NANCY: *(Surprised)* Why not ?

SHEKHAR: The Government of India won't permit you.

NANCY: Why ?

SHEKHAR: Foreigners need a special permit to go to Assam.

The Announcer's voice came on the microphone ...

ANNOUNCER: Now we come to the most important item of this evening "The Breaking of the Chains" where our most beloved friend, Laxmi, plays the role of "Mother India" ...

Reena looked around to see if Neel had come. The man who tried to take Neel's seat was talking loudly to Reena. Reena replied equally rudely and kept possession of the seat.

The curtain opened. Laxmi, dressed in an exquisite sari, was standing on a pedestal in front of the map of India. She was playing the role of "Mother India" in some stage prop looking like a chain. Other boys and girls, dressed as fighters in the struggle for independence, sang and marched around her, bringing the reminiscence of the shooting at Jalinwalabagh, marching of British troops, hanging of some freedom fighters, Mahatma Gandhi's Salt March, etc. Laxmi was in the middle of the

85

stage, on the small pedestal, in front of the map of India. Her chains were now gone. The revolutionaries knelt down to her, sang "Vandey Maataram", meaning "I adore you, my Mother !", the old song of the revolutionaries who died for the freedom of India.

Nancy was looking at Laxmi, spell bound.

NANCY: She is beautiful !

SHEKHAR: So is Mother India in our imagination.

In the taxi ride back to her International Students' Hostel, Nancy had many questions for Shekhar.

NANCY: *(Continuing ...)* So, what's the meaning of the word Laxmi ?

SHEKHAR: Laxmi is the name of a goddess. The goddess of wealth, peace, well-being and beauty. She has many names like Iswari, Kamla, Laxmi, Achala, ...

NANCY: *(Interrupting)* Wait a minute, did you say Kamla ?

SHEKHAR: *(A pause)* Yes.

NANCY: That was the name of your wife.

SHEKHAR: *(A pause)* Yes. *(After some self-control)* These are very popular names. Many girls are given these names, with the hope that there will be wealth, well-being, peace and love and beauty in their lives ...

The taxi stopped in front of a building with a sign, "INTERNATIONAL STUDENTS' HOSTEL". Nancy got out.

NANCY: *(Bending over the taxi door)* So, you're going to bring the two cassettes of the Gandhi movie for me ?

SHEKHAR: Yes. Tomorrow. I know someone who has it.

NANCY: And I know somebody in our hostel who has a VCR. Thanks, Shekhar. See you tomorrow.

Back in Meredith Hotel, Jim, Willy and Bob were in the middle of many problems.

JIM: I still believe you should have waited for Shekhar.

WILLY: How could I wait any longer ? They wanted a reply today !

BOB: And, what precisely did they say in the Embassy ?

WILLY: They said all mountaineering is suspended. As they said in the letter, we have to go back.

Willy passed over a letter to Jim and Bob.

BOB: This must be some kind of politics by the Royal Geographic people.

JIM: Must we blame our competition all the time ? There may be some way out. Shekhar warned us about unforeseen problems, I'm sure he'll be able to solve ...

WILLY: But, he's not here, what can we do ?

JIM: He got all government permissions. This is his department.

BOB: I'm sure they will lift the ban as soon as the Royal Geographic guys send their team of climbers.

A knock at the door. Bob opened. Shekhar was at the door.

WILLY: Where you have been last two days ?

BOB: We've a big problem here.

SHEKHAR: What ?

WILLY: Read it for yourself.

Bob passed the letter to Shekhar.

JIM: Well, you're in charge of Government permissions. It's your problem now.

Shekhar read the letter.

SHEKHAR: What's the problem ?

WILLY: Didn't you read it ? No permission for mountaineering ?

SHEKHAR: This is a copy of an old order. Who gave you this ?

WILLY: What ? They gave it to me in the Nepal Embassy yesterday.

SHEKHAR: Nepalese Embassy ? Was it the main building ?

WILLY: No, not the main building, it's a kind of annex
...

SHEKHAR: Two miles from the main office of the
Embassy ?

WILLY: Yes. Do you know where it is ?

SHEKHAR: Yes, I do. I went there before. This order
has been superseded. Did you pay any money to them ?

WILLY: No ! Why should I ?

SHEKHAR: Don't ask those questions. Do you want to
go to Nepal ? I've the permissions in my suitcase over
there.

He pointed to a couple of suitcases at one corner
of the room.

JIM: How much did you pay in bribes ?

SHEKHAR: Five thousand rupees. They must have tried
to get some more money from Willy.

BOB: How strange !

SHEKHAR: The only problem is that we must have a
medical doctor in our team before we actually start
climbing, that's a major condition.

JIM: Can we get a doctor to join us over here ?

SHEKHAR: I'll try. But, there isn't much time. We must leave as soon as possible, before they give us another hard time.

JIM: How can we possibly do that if you keep on vanishing for long hours like this.

SHEKHAR: I had to go to see Nancy.

WILLY: Forget about Nancy, she's a big girl, she does not need your chaperoning !

JIM: Has she cooled down a little bit ?

SHEKHAR: Outside, yes. Inside, I don't know. But, the real danger is coming from Neel.

WILLY: Neel ??

SHEKHAR: Neel thinks that I am instigating Nancy to go against him, so he will take revenge on all of us.

BOB: Like what ?

SHEKHAR: He left the message with a common friend that if Nancy intervenes in his wedding, he will fax all the papers to London.

JIM: What ?

SHEKHAR: The common friend didn't understand what's this all about. But, I think, if Nancy fouls up with the wedding, Neel will fax those calculations to Royal Geographic Society.

Everybody swore.

WILLY: That'll be the end of his life.

BOB: All that we wanted is to climb a mountain. Now, all these politics !

SHEKHAR: I'm trying to meet Neel. I'm in close contact with Nancy. You guys get ready. We must go to Kathmandu as soon as possible.

Nancy did not know that Neel was avoiding her. She also did not know that Neel had, by this time, indoctrinated his family with his side of the story about her. She went to Neel's house one more time. Neel heard the knock and came to open the door. Then, suddenly, he saw Nancy through the window. He froze just before opening the door. In quick movements, he turned around and ran to Reena. He whispered something to Reena, ran to the backyard, opened the door at the perimeter wall, went out to the road, stopped a cruising three-wheeler taxi, and rushed off. Nancy knocked at the front door again. Reena opened the door and greeted Nancy hypocritically ...

REENA: Oh, Nancy ! Come'n in !

Reena ushered Nancy to their living room. Tara came to join them.

TARA: I'm sorry, Neel is not home today also !

REENA: He went out in the morning.

NANCY: I've brought some more perfumes, maybe you'll like them !

TARA: The other day, you didn't take tea with us. You must take some tea today ! You're just like my daughter, you know ! *(Shouted for Sona)* Sona, Sona, bring some tea !

NANCY: Sona is home today ?

TARA: Oh, yeah ! Reena, will you go and see what she's doing !

Reena went to the kitchen.

TARA: India is not the same as before. The servants have become so notorious these days ...

NANCY: *(With some surprise)* Servants ? Did you see the Gandhi movie ?

TARA: Oh, yes ! At Prime Minister's house ! My husband is a senior worker for the Prime Minister's party. All our neighbors are so jealous of us ! The movie was s----o good ! Everybody wept. Even the Prime Minister wept. My daughter, Reena, wept more than anybody else.

Sona entered with a tray of tea. Thinking that it would be wise to follow what Mahatma Gandhi did in Mr. Jinna's house in the movie "Gandhi", Nancy got up and took the tray from Sona. Everybody was surprised.

NANCY: *(To Sona)* Would you please !

REENA: *(To Nancy, in great surprise)* What are you doing ?

    Nancy served tea to everybody.

TARA: You don't have to say "please" to a servant like that !

NANCY: *(Surprised)* I thought ... you said you liked the Gandhi movie ?

    Nancy held Sona by her hand and made her sit down with her. Sona was never allowed to seat on the sofa. She looked at Tara and Reena in great confusion.

NANCY: *(To Sona)* You have such a cute, sweet face ! You will look beautiful if you wear good clothes !

    Sona's mouth opened in surprise. She got some kind of a confidence. With a child's curiosity, she asked ...

SONA: You think so ?

NANCY: Where did you learn English ?

SONA: Kornel Uncle taught us.

TARA: *(Enraged)* There's an ostracized Army Colonel in our neighborhood, you know ! He and his wife are spoiling all our servants.

REENA: They keep on inciting these ordinary people ...

NANCY: *(To Sona, noticing the scar on one side of her face)* What happened here ?

Sona gave a look towards Tara and Reena. Suddenly, a spirit of defiance came to her. She was not as afraid as she was supposed to be. In an icy tone, she said ...

SONA: Nothing.

Sona hesitated for a second, then took out her doll from her waitress pocket and showed it to Nancy ...

SONA: Do you like this ?

NANCY: That's a beautiful doll ! Where did you get it ?

SONA: *(Proudly)* I made it.

NANCY: *(Surprised)* You made it ? Where did you learn to make dolls ?

SONA: Kornel Uncle and Aunt taught us. Would you like to see them ?

NANCY: Would you take me to them ?

SONA: Yes. Please come with me !

Sona led Nancy to the back door. Tara shouted ...

TARA: Sona, you have a lot of dishes to do !

NANCY: *(To Tara)* I'll come and help her with the dishes, if you want ! We wont be long, anyway !

Tara's mouth opened in surprise. She kept on looking at the receding figures of Nancy and Sona. Reena joined Tara and said jeeringly ...

REENA: These low-born Americans ! She must be from some ordinary family.

TARA: But, *(in a confused tone)* she gave us a lot of expensive perfumes !

On the back porch of Mr. Saxena's house, his wife, Karuna, an elderly lady in a sari, was teaching doll making to a couple of thirteen year old servant girls who were virtually in rags. Two boys, the same age, in rags, were learning English from Mr. Saxena. Sona introduced Nancy very excitedly.

SONA: Uncle-ji, Aunt-ji, see ... please see ... who is here ! She is the one I told you about ! She thinks I'll be beautiful if I get good clothes !

KARUNA: Of course you'll be beautiful. In fact, you're already beautiful. So are Anuradha and Kanti !

The other two girls blushed at the mention of their names.

SAXENA: And Ahmed and Rakhal are doing very good in their studies !

The two boys smiled happily at the recognition.

Saxena took them all to the living room. It was a hot day. Karuna went to the kitchen to make laschi, aided by the children.

SAXENA: When I told Sona to call you here if you visit them again, I didn't have the slightest idea that you also came to see Doctor Sharma in this country ! What a strange coincidence ! Or, maybe not. Doctor Sharma is a very famous man by his own rights.

NANCY: I have an address here. Do you think I can find him there ?

SAXENA: Nobody knows. However, you should check it out. If you find him, give him my regards. Please tell him, I'll ever be grateful to him for his article.

NANCY: What was that ?

SAXENA: When the top brass of the Indian Army forced me to go on retirement, he was the only journalist who supported me.

NANCY: Why ? Why they ...

SAXENA: *(With the impatience of an old man)* I was

ordered to make an enquiry. I did my job. When I submitted my report, my superior told me to change my report.

NANCY: What was that all about ?

SAXENA: Well, it's a shameful story. I am an army officer, I'm proud of the Indian Army. In the Second World War, the Indian Army was regarded as one of the finest armies in the entire world. But, the Indian Army is as big and as vast as the Indian Nation. There may be one or two dirty officers, or one or two dirty battalions. Our job is to make enquiry and punish the guilty, so that the name of the Army is held untarnished.

NANCY: What happened ?

SAXENA: There were reports that one battalion of the Army committed massive rape in the North Kamrup district of Assam. Some news papers published the reports in their back pages, because it is considered unpatriotic to write anything against the Army. However, the Government was forced to make an enquiry. I was posted in New Delhi at that time. I was deputed to make the enquiry. At the beginning, I did not believe those news reports and went there with a lot of incredulity. But, when I interviewed those women ...

NANCY: *(Surprised)* Those women came out to give testimony in an open enquiry ?

SAXENA: Yes. They were peasant women. Honor is a matter of life and death for them. They were extremely angry. It was alleged there were as many as one hundred and fifty cases. I recorded forty-nine affidavits. The stories were ghastly. One young mother told me, she clutched on to her eight month old baby in her arms when the soldiers broke into her house, tied up her husband and tore off her clothes. One soldier snatched the baby away and threw the baby to the ceiling.

NANCY: The baby died ?

SAXENA: An old woman came to see me. She was some eighty years old. Her hands were in plaster. Her back also was broken. She virtually crawled. Her bones were broken by the strong and valiant soldiers of the Indian Army, because she tried to save her daughter-in-law. On and on and on. Forty-nine cases. I couldn't eat or sleep those days. Shame, shame, shame, ... that I belonged to the same Army. I was so angry. I was absolutely determined to punish the guilty. But, when I submitted the report, General Dutta ordered me that I must withdraw the report. When I asked why, he said that Prime Minister did not want the report to be written that way. He told me to write another report exonerating all wrong doing by the Army. I refused. He shouted at me, calling me names, saying that I had been anti-national and extremely unpatriotic to give such a bad name to the army ....

　　Mr. Saxena paused.

NANCY: What did you say ?

SAXENA: I asked calmly, "What about those women ? Do you think they were raped very patriotically ?"

NANCY: And, ... your report ?

SAXENA: I didn't withdraw my report. So, I was forced to retire from the Armed Services ...

NANCY: What happened to the report ?

SAXENA: They hushed it up. When Doctor Sharma published an article and demanded a copy of the report, they raided his printing press, destroyed all equipment and supplies, beat up the employees, burnt the place down ...

NANCY: They means who ?

SAXENA: It's complicated. People say it was done by the Prime Minister's party workers, but, the Police was the inactive observer. Some witnesses will say Police helped the so-called party workers.

NANCY: Why the Army was sent to Assam in the first place ?

SAXENA: Because the citizens of that state made a non-violent protest against holding any election with a voters' list that contained millions of names of foreigners from East Pakistan.

NANCY: Why should the Prime Minister approve that list ?

SAXENA: Nobody knows. Maybe she thinks these Pakistani muslims will vote for her party.

NANCY: It's very complicated.

SAXENA: Go and meet Doctor Sharma. When I met him, I was amazed to see the level of his study. He should be able to clear up your questions.

NANCY: I'll definitely meet him. But, why did you call me ?

SAXENA: I wanted to give you a copy of my original report. Newspapers here are afraid to publish that report. Maybe you can get it published in the USA.

Saxena got up and brought the report from a drawer.

NANCY: Will it help you if it is published ?

SAXENA: No. On the contrary, they'll take revenge on me. They'll find out some way to finish me.

NANCY: Oh my God ! You've already suffered a lot. Why do you want to do it ?

SAXENA: To uphold truth. Truth is very powerful. That's the light we saw ... thousands of years ago ... in Mundaka Upanishad. We may suffer on our journey, but at the end, truth will triumph.

Makkhanlal, Neel's father, an elderly man, was watching Nancy from the porch of his house next door. He was being briefed by his daughter, Reena, who was pointing at Nancy as she came out of Saxena's house to her taxi.

REENA: That's the girl, that's the girl. Papa, you must do something.

MAKKHANLAL: I've already informed Phulraj Mathur. He'll be here any minute. Look, she's going back to the house !

REENA: Yeah ! She forgot something, I think.

An expensive Mercedes stopped in front of Neel's house. Phulraj Mathur, a middle aged man, with an authoritative look, emerged from the Mercedes. Makkhanlal and Reena virtually ran to the car.

REENA: O Uncle-ji, you are right in time ...

MAKKHANLAL: Namastey *(meaning "Welcome")* Mathur Sahib !

The three came to the porch. They watched Nancy coming out, followed by Saxena, who said good-bye to her. Nancy and Saxena did not see that Reena, Makkhanlal and Phulraj were watching.

A serious conference started at the living room of Neel's house. Phulraj and Makkhanlal were seated on sofa, sipping tea. Tara and Reena were in attendance.

PHULRAJ: Then, what happened ?

TARA: Then, Colonel Saxena pushed me and Reena on the ground and took away that despicable servant girl ...

PHULRAJ: Do you think the girl will give witness against the Colonel ?

REENA: She will, if you give money to her father in the village ...

MAKKHANLAL: She may not, because the Colonel is popular, he gives love, not only to her, but to all servants in the neighborhood ...

TARA: *(To Makkhanlal)* You keep quiet ! You're the one who went on tolerating the Colonel and playing between me and the servant ...

PHULRAJ: Well, Tara-ji, it'll be difficult to prove the assault charge against the Colonel. His Army record is spotless. In the 1965 War, when he was only a young Lieutenant of Artillery, he was named "Karak Bijli" "The Thunderbolt Cannon" in the Western Front. In the 1971 War, he was specially commissioned by General Aurora. We had a hard time even retiring him from the Army. We've got to be careful. The political situation is very touchy at this time. Mata-ji *(meaning Indira Gandhi, respectfully)* told me to be very careful. But, if that American girl keeps on coming to see him, we may try him as a CIA agent.

REENA: *(Excitedly)* Well, we'll immediately inform you when that American girl sees him next time.

PHULRAJ: That may be a good idea. But, don't do anything now. I'll have to talk to Mata-ji before that.

MAKKHANLAL: I still don't have the telephone.

PHULRAJ: How come ?

Makkhanlal shrugged.

PHULRAJ: You talk to Mr. Shrivastav in the telephone department. Tell him I told you.

MAKKHANLAL: Oh, thank you, thank you !

PHULRAJ: Now, Tara-ji, Reena, will you please excuse us, I've got to talk privately with Makkhanlal.

TARA: Oh, of course. I shall be in the kitchen. Call me if you need anything.

Tara went to the kitchen, followed by Reena. Makkhanlal got up and closed all the doors.

PHULRAJ: Well, Makkhanlal-ji, the political situation is very troublesome at this time. Mata-ji is very worried.

MAKKHANLAL: About the Sikh problem ?

PHULRAJ: *(Yawning)* Yeah, the Sikh problem in the West, the Assam problem in the East ... but the biggest problem is ... the Hindu problem in mainland.

MAKKHANLAL: Hindu problem ? We never had a Hindu problem ! The Hindus are divided people, they lost all their character in seven hundred years of the Islamic Rule. The Hindus can be purchased, can be divided, can be traded, can be bent in any direction you want ... they're no problem !

PHULRAJ: Not any more ! You know that our stronghold is the Muslim vote. Do you know what'll happen to us if the Hindus get united ?

MAKKHANLAL: *(Horrified)* Oh my God ! We'll be finished !

PHULRAJ: That's exactly what is happening. All those marches of mass people, the Virat Hindu Samaj marches, the combined leadership of the Gurus, ... Now Mata-ji is thinking of making friends with the Hindus.

MAKKHANLAL: Well, that shouldn't be difficult. Get some Muslims killed. The Hindus will then become friendly to Mata-ji's government.

PHULRAJ: That's not possible. If Muslims are killed, the Arab countries will go against her. Money is needed for the elections. Mata-ji can't afford to upset the Arab financiers at this time.

MAKKHANLAL: What's the solution, then ?

PHULRAJ: Sikhs.

MAKKHANLAL: Sikhs ?

PHULRAJ: Yeah. Sikhs. We've to divert the Hindu anger towards the Sikhs.

MAKKHANLAL: How's that possible ? Hindus and Sikhs are the same people ! They worship the same Goddess Chandee ... that's how starts the Great Holy Book of the Sikhs ...

PHULRAJ: Forget about the Holy Book ! Who reads the holy book, anyway ? People go by their sentiments.

MAKKHANLAL: It'll be difficult to split the Hindus and the Sikhs at this time, Mathur Sahib ! Particularly after the shooting last week in Amritsar, where Sikhs had a non-violent demonstration and the Government opened fire, killing four Sikhs ...

PHULRAJ: Do you know what I need to split the Sikhs and Hindus ?

107

MAKKHANLAL: What ?

PHULRAJ: Two heads of cows.

MAKKHANLAL: *(Shouted in great distress)* What ?

PHULRAJ: Don't shout. Put your Hindu taboos away.

MAKKHANLAL: Two heads of cows ??

PHULRAJ: Yes. Two heads of cows. Two heads of cows will be found in front of a Hindu temple one morning. Then, Mataji will go to the Parliament and give a statement that Sikhs were responsible.

Makkhanlal cooled down at the mention of the name of Mataji.

MAKKHANLAL: Well, that may work. Cows are sacred for the Hindus. If you can convince the Hindus that the Sikhs did it, Sikhs will be butchered by the Hindus. But, how will you do that in the Sikh capital, Amritsar ? Sikhs do not kill cows ! Cows are as much holy to the Sikhs as they're to the Hindus. How do you find two cow-heads in Amritsar ?

PHULRAJ: Can you go to Amritsar in the next two or three days ?

MAKKHANLAL: To arrange for two cow heads ? *(In great distress)* Mathur Sahib, I'm a Hindu Brahmin, and you want me to do this ?

PHULRAJ: It's for the sake of our political Party, Makkhanlal, it is to save our political power in the Government. You must put your taboos aside.

MAKKHANLAL: I understand. But, *(a pause)* this is too much, don't tell Mata-ji, I don't want to be out of her favor, but this is too much for me !

PHULRAJ: *(After a pause)* All right. I'll get Mr. Chabra do it.

MAKKHANLAL: But,... how will he do it ? He's a vegetarian, too !

PHULRAJ: He'll have to get a Muslim butcher to kill the cows.

MAKKHANLAL: A Muslim butcher ? He'll kill the animal in halal ... cutting a small piece of the throat at a time, that's awful !

Phulraj was visibly annoyed. In a harsh voice he said, "Don't worry about it, Makkhanlal ! But there's something that you can do for the Party. We need some call-girls for the Assam boys."

MAKKHANLAL: Assam boys ?

PHULRAJ: Yes. The student leaders of Assam Movement are in Delhi for negotiation. We tried to bribe them with foreign gifts, but they wouldn't accept it. We tried to move them to luxurious hotels, they refused. We offered money, they refused. We doubled and tripled the money.

Can you believe it, they still refused. So, we're going to try something that a young man cannot refuse.

MAKKHANLAL: And, *(a pause)* You want me to arrange for call girls ... *(a pause)* I am a Brahmin, Mathur Sahib ....

PHULRAJ: *(Shouting)* You're a Brahmin, I'm a Kayastha, we're all high caste Hindus ! But, this is politics, Makkhanlal, and somebody has to do these things ... *(a pause)* All right, I'll ask Chabra to do it. You tell me what you can do, and when you can do it. What happened to the dowry of your son's wedding ? Did Mr. Kishore Dwivedi pay you ?

MAKKHANLAL: He paid only one lakh. He was supposed to pay three lakhs in advance.

PHULRAJ: What does he say ?

MAKKHANLAL: The same old story. He would pay some money at the Tilak. He'd pay some more at the Godbhari. Then, he'd pay some more at the wedding. And the balance within three months.

PHULRAJ: That's not fair. He promised you six lakh of rupees to catch your boy, and now he's doing this ?

MAKKHANLAL: What can I do, Sahib ! Is there any goodness left in this world ?!

It was an unidentifiable backyard, cut off from the neighborhood by a high wall. Time was evening. Phulraj and Chabra were busy supervising the beheading of two cows. Chabra was a well-built man, much younger than Phulraj. The headless carcass of one cow was on the ground. Its severed head was on a bench. The other cow was being slaughtered by the "Halal" (kosher) rules. The butcher cut the animal's throat a few inches at a time. The animal was in great anguish. The butcher finally severed the head and put both the heads in a sack. Chabra handed out a bundle of money to the butcher. A bearded man took charge of the sack. Chabra handed out a few more bundle of money to the bearded man.

PHULRAJ: *(To Chabra)* Do you think his beards are full enough to pass for a Sikh ?

CHABRA: Sure. *(To the bearded man)* Now you put on a turban like a Sikh. Remember, you must dump the cow-heads in front of the temple early in the morning, so that the priest will see you and think that you are a Sikh.

BEARDED MAN: Yes Sir !

PHULRAJ: You'll get rest of the money after the job is done. Now, rush. You must drive three hundred miles to Amritsar in one night.

BEARDED MAN: No problem, Sir !

The man left with the sack in his hand. Phulraj watched him go. He sighed involuntarily, "The two cows were absolutely innocent."

CHABRA: Two cows and four girls.

PHULRAJ: That makes six of them.

CHABRA: Why did you order for only four call-girls ? I heard the number of student leaders in the Assam team is eight.

PHULRAJ: That's right. I want them to fight amongst themselves.

CHABRA: That's a smart idea. Anyway, the girls are waiting for you. Would you like to check ...

PHULRAJ: I don't have to check. You're expert in those kind of things. Only make sure that the secret photographs come out all right. We may have to use those photographs if the political negotiation doesn't go as per the plan.

CHABRA: *(Shook his head)* Last time I supplied call-girls for that Middle-East Delegation, I got blamed that they were not attractive. You must come and check if the things are all right this time.

What followed next was a disgusting scene in a secret room somewhere in Old Delhi. Chabra and Phulraj checked the skin, flesh and limbs of the call-girls. They rejected two girls who had to be replaced by two other girls with better endowment of flesh.

It was late that evening when the car arrived the Assam House with the girls. Assam House was the official boarding house where the delegation from Assam were accommodated. The student leaders from Assam were in a late-night discussion in a conference room, getting ready for their tough negotiation with the Prime Minister next morning. The girls entered with trays of drinks and snacks. Gogoi, the chief of the student leaders, asked, "Are these alcohol ?"

Rekha, one of the girls, replied, "Yes ! You'll like them …"

GOGOI: *(Authoritatively)* No. Take them back. We have a very serious negotiation tomorrow morning.

REKHA: We've have soft drinks also. Will you like some soft drink ?

GOGOI: That's what I ordered.

Rekha, aided by the other girls, poured soft drink in glasses with a lot of sex appeal.

REKHA: Here's your soft drink. And a plenty of soft flesh, if you care to enjoy ...

Gogoi stood up. He questioned Rekha in a very stern voice ...

GOGOI: Who are you ?

REKHA: You can find that out by removing my blouse !

All the girls giggled.

GOGOI: *(To the girls, in extreme anger)* Will you get out, all of you ? We have an important negotiation tomorrow morning ... which is life and death of our people ...

REKHA: *(Taken aback, but she still tried)* We know. But, that's in the morning. Now, it's night. You're young. You should enjoy life.

GOGOI: Life ? We don't have any life. We're dead people. Our homes and hearths have been overrun by a civilian invasion of foreigners. We appealed to our government in a non-violent protest, we were shot and our mothers and sisters were raped.

All other members of the delegation were looking at Gogoi. The girls left the room, dismayed, faces down.

It was early in the morning when the bearded man arrived at the Hindu temple in Amritsar. The man had sported a turban and looked like a Sikh. The temple door was open. The Priest was singing the morning prayers inside the temple. He was a thin, underfed man. His ribs could be counted, but he had a serene face and a sonorous, musical voice. He was singing the morning prayers in the music of the exquisite Raga Bhairava. He had his back towards the porch. The bearded man waited at the porch with the sack in his hand.

When the Priest finished his prayers and came out to the porch, the Bearded Man unloaded the cow-heads on the porch and waited nervously. The Priest saw the cow-heads, shouted and went berserk, pointing to the Bearded Man deliriously. Now the Bearded Man turned around and ran in circles so that everyone would see him. Some bystanders chased him. The Bearded Man vanished at a bend.

Next day, Nancy went to the Meredith Hotel to meet Shekhar. She found him reading a news paper with a big news about rioting between Hindus and Sikhs. The rioting started after the Prime Minister delivered a speech in the Parliament that Sikhs were responsible for throwing two cow heads at a Hindu temple in Amritsar.

NANCY: It's a mess.

SHEKHAR: I agree with you.

NANCY: How come India has such a high philosophy and such a low ... such a low ...

SHEKHAR: I don't know the answer.

NANCY: I must go and ask Doctor Sharma.

SHEKHAR: No, Nancy ! In my very humble opinion, you should go back to the United States. Forget Neel. He doesn't deserve you. Go and live your own life.

NANCY: When are you guys leaving for Kathmandu ?

SHEKHAR: We're leaving in a day or two. I'd like to put you on a flight to New York today, if you agree.

NANCY: *(Got up)* Thanks. I'll go back after I finish my work.

SHEKHAR: But, you said you don't have any grudge against Neel's bride.

NANCY: That's right. She is innocent.

SHEKHAR: So, you can now go home.

NANCY: Not so soon. I've to find the real culprit.

Shekhar went on staring at Nancy. What would be her plan ? Would she go after Neel now ? This was a new turn in the problem and he did not know how to tackle it.

But, Nancy did not think of Neel at that time. She thought she was witnessing something much greater than Neel's pettiness. She would have to meet Dr. Kilgore's friend, she thought.

After a few days, with Doctor Sharma's address in her hand, Nancy went in a narrow path somewhere in the outskirts of Delhi. She stopped a man and asked, "Do you know which is the house of Doctor Sharma ?"

The man gave a fearful look at Nancy, turned around and ran away. Nancy was surprised. She went on watching the receding figure of the man. She walked a little further, trying to locate a number on the houses in consultation with a little note that she was carrying. She asked another man, "Do you know which is the house of Doctor Sharma ?"

This man also gave a fearful look at Nancy, turned around and started to run away. Nancy was very surprised.

"Wait a minute !", she shouted, "All that I want is to see Doctor Sharma !"

Nancy realized instinctively that somebody was observing her from behind a half closed window. With her characteristic stubbornness, she walked to that house and knocked loudly at the door, "Anybody in ?"

The door opened. Sneha, a young woman of Nancy's age, with a large burn mark on her right face and neck, was at the door.

SNEHA: I heard you were asking for Doctor Sharma ?

NANCY: Yes !

SNEHA: Please come in !

Sneha's living room did not have sofas. There were a few wooden chairs.

SNEHA: It's dangerous to ask about Doctor Sharma like that.

NANCY: That's why those men ran away ?

SNEHA: Yes.

NANCY: Why ?

SNEHA: Because Doctor Sharma got into trouble with the Prime Minister. All his associates are being rounded up one by one.

NANCY: Did you know him ?

SNEHA: I used to work for him. He taught me every-thing. His printing press was next door. I could go there early in the morning and come home late at night, so that nobody could see my face.

NANCY: Excuse me, ... please ... what happened to your face ? Why do you try to hide it ?

SNEHA: I don't hide it any more. I am going to fight for it.

NANCY: What happened ?

SNEHA: You will not understand. Did you ever hear that young brides are burnt in India if their parents can't pay dowry money ?

Nancy gasped.

NANCY: My God ! So ... you were burnt by your in-laws ?

SNEHA: I didn't die. The nurses in the Delhi Hospital Burn Center saved my life.

NANCY: I want to find out everything about it.

SNEHA: Why ?

NANCY: I will find out and fight. The Government of India will have to do something about it.

SNEHA: There is an anti-dowry law in India. But nothing works. It's a very deep rooted social evil.

NANCY: Well, I'll publish the news in America. When the whole world will know, it will stop ...

SNEHA: Some TV people came from America and took pictures. Doctor Sharma sent me to help them. Did you see those pictures ?

NANCY: You're talking about the CBS show, Sixty Minutes ? I didn't see it, but I heard about it. Where can I find Doctor Sharma ?

SNEHA: I don't know. After his printing press was broken down, he went into hiding. Some people say he fled to Nepal.

NANCY: To Kathmandu ?

SNEHA: Kathmandu is the capital of Nepal. But, I don't know whether he is there.

NANCY: Is there any way I could get to the Delhi Hospital Burn Center ? I want to interview some patients.

SNEHA: You must be very careful there. The Hospital doesn't want to give out any information.

NANCY: Why ? Why all this secrecy ?

SNEHA: I don't know. I think they don't want to tarnish the image of India.

By this time, the two men who ran away from Nancy had arrived at their destination, the Police Station. A junior constable walked to the Police Officer on duty and saluted.

CONSTABLE: Informer number twenty-seven and twenty-nine at the door, sir !

OFFICER: Bring them in.

The Constable went out and returned with the two men. They were very timid and shaken. They saluted the officer repeatedly.

INFORMER: American girl asking about Sharma, sir !

The Officer shouted and stood up in great excitement ...

OFFICER: What ? American girl ?

INFORMER: Yes sir. Very white.

The Officer reached for his telephone, dialed some numbers and started to talk to his immediate superior.

OFFICER: Yes, sir ! American girl, that's what the informer number twenty-seven said. Very white.

When his immediate superior got that message, it started a chain reaction in the police department. Many Police Officers were talking on telephones, one by one, each reporting, by using the word "sir" umpteen number of times, to his superior that an American girl ... ultimate proof of CIA connections ... was looking for Sharma. This was followed by the inevitable climax: A platoon of Policemen, marching on foot, led by an Officer in an open Jeep, left the Police Station, similar to the Jalinwalabag expedition of General Dyer in the Gandhi movie.

Unaware of the imminent danger, Nancy was talking to Sneha in Sneha's house. A bond of natural friendship was building up between them.

NANCY: How do you propose to fight ?

SNEHA: I don't know. Sharma-ji was our leader in all our fights against social injustice. Now he is gone. Some Women's Organizations helped the TV group that came from the USA. We're trying to reorganize them. It is difficult. There are too many divided opinions. Some people try to avoid all publicity. But, how can you fight something like this without publicity ?

NANCY: I don't understand that at all.

SNEHA: I had a friend, from my childhood days, Seeta ... she became a doctor and was posted in the Burn Center. I told her to keep a record of those cases which can be suspected as dowry burning.

NANCY: *(Excitedly)* Oh, those records will be invaluable !

SNEHA: But, she refused. She said she would have to ask her boss.

NANCY: Why ?

SNEHA: Everybody is afraid of something ... I don't

know why !

NANCY: But, what about the victims ? We can take statements from those girls who are half burnt, who are in pain ...

SNEHA: Some of them may give testimony. But, you'll be surprised, most of them will not. Even I didn't, at the beginning. I thought ... I hoped ... I would be accepted some day ... after all my sufferings.

NANCY: But, ... *(A pause)* ... you were not ?

SNEHA: *(Shook her head)* I am not afraid any more.

Both became silent for a while. Sneha broke the silence by asking softly, "Have you heard about Mother Ayesha ?"

NANCY: No ! Who is she ?

SNEHA: She is from some Arab country. She runs a Convent here. They help the homeless girls. I was there for some time. Then, Doctor Sharma gave me the job in his printing shop.

Suddenly, a flash of anger crossed Nancy's mind. Her cheeks and ears became red. In a hoarse voice, she took leadership, "All right, Sneha ! Please try to find out where is Doctor Sharma. And, let us go to the Burn Center. I must see what's going on there."

The platoon of policemen, marching behind the slow-moving jeep of the Police Officer, arrived at the narrow road. A crowd gathered. They saw Nancy and Sneha come out from the house. The Officer spotted Nancy. He yelled some orders. The Policemen stopped, saw and ran to surround Nancy. Sneha covered Nancy, shouting ...

SNEHA: *(Shouted)* No, no, no, you can't take her ...

Sneha placed herself between Police and Nancy, spreading her arms to shield Nancy. The Officer gave a full slap on Sneha's face. She fell down on the ground.

OFFICER: Arrest them. Both of them.

The police hustled Nancy and Sneha onto the jeep. The jeep backed a long distance because there was no place to turn the vehicle in that narrow road.

At the Police Station, Nancy took a surprisingly authoritative stance. She told the Duty Officer, "Now that you have our names and identifications, I want to see Mister Dixit."

The Duty Officer was very surprised.

Duty Officer: Dixit ? Who Dixit ?

NANCY: The Police Chief. Mr. Roshan Dixit.

The Duty Officer panicked. If this girl knew the Police Chief personally ...

Duty Officer: You want to see Dixit Sahib ? Why ?

NANCY: *(Sternly)* Never mind why. Call him and give him my name.

The Duty Officer dialed the telephone, and talked to his superior nervously. His superior ran into a panic, "She wants to see Dixit ? Why ? ... Oh my God ... wait a minute, let me ask my boss ... "

When his immediate superior got that message, it started a chain reaction in the police department. Many Police Officers were talking on telephones, one by one, each reporting, by using the word "sir" umpteen number of times, to his superior that an American girl ... a veritable proof of CIA connections ... was looking for the Police Chief, Roshan Dixit.

In the long hallway of the Police Headquarters, top floor, Nancy and Sneha were walking, led by Ashok, a young Police Officer in full uniform, apparently a new recruit, and followed by two police men. They stopped in front of a door marked "ROSHAN DIXIT, I.P.S., CHIEF OF POLICE". With all the energy and enthusiasm of a new recruit, Ashok knocked at the door. Mr. Dixit's voice: "Come in."

Ashok opened the door and saluted. Dixit's voice was very courteous, "You all stay outside. I'll have to talk to Nancy in private."

Dixit escorted Nancy to his desk.

NANCY: You know my name ?

DIXIT: You knew my name, didn't you ? It's from the same source, your uncle, Mr. Agnitti. Please be seated.

NANCY: You know my uncle ?

DIXIT: By telephone. I'm supposed to ring him up when I see you. What time it will be in the United States at this time ?

He started dialing some numbers on the telephone.

NANCY: Why did your men arrest me ?

DIXIT: *(Very apologetically)* Oh, that was a mistake. A grave error. You are free to go wherever you want to.

NANCY: Why did they slap Sneha ? She's the nicest girl ...

128

DIXIT: *(Interrupting)* Oh, don't worry about her, these are ordinary people, she comes from the homeless center of Mother Ayesha ...

Dixit now started to talk into the telephone.

DIXIT: *(To the telephone)* Yes, may I talk to Mr. Agnitti ... *(Pause)* ... yes Mr. Agnitti, sorry to bother you at this hour, but you told me to ring you no matter what's the time ...

At the other end of the telephone, in Boston North End, Mr. Agnitti was taking the call very seriously.

AGNITTI: *(To the telephone)* Never mind the time ... *(Pause)* ... Is Nancy over there ? ... *(Pause)* ... Yes, I'll talk to her later, let me first bring your son to the telephone, please hold ...

Agnitti pressed the "hold" button and dialed a few numbers.

AGNITTI: *(To the telephone)* Tony, pick up the phone ... where are you ?

Tony, one of the bodyguards of Agnitti, took the call at his car parked near a building with a sign "LIBRARY: HARVARD UNIVERSITY".

TONY: *(To the telephone)* I'm in front of the library, Boss !

AGNITTI: *(At his end of the telephone)* Where is the rabbit ?

TONY: The rabbit is inside the Library.

AGNITTI: Do you have somebody watching the rabbit inside the Library ?

TONY: Nick and Bryan are watching him.

AGNITTI: Bring him to your telephone.

Tony was now speaking to his walkie-talkie.

TONY: Nick !

Nick was inside the library. He was pretending to read a book .... something that he never liked to do in his entire life ... in one table, overlooking Bryan and Harish who were at another table. Harish was reading and making some notes. Bryan was pretending to read, but actually he was watching Harish.

Nick's walkie-talkie looked like a walk-man with earphones ... a very common item in the student community. He spoke to the mouth-piece.

NICK: Yeah !

TONY: *(To the walkie-talkie)* Bring the rabbit to my car.

Nick signalled Bryan. Bryan got up and signalled Harish to come. Harish got up in utter panic. He looked around and saw Nick was standing just behind him. All the three walked out from the library and approached Tony's car.

At Mr. Dixit's room, he was trying his best to conceal his nervousness. He talked a little more than what he would talk normally ... "Your uncle wanted to talk to you, but then he told me to hold. It's almost midnight in Boston at this time. Did you know my son studies in Boston these days ? He took transfer from Yale to Harvard. Your uncle helped him to get the transfer. Apparently your uncle has immense influence with these universities .... "

Ten thousand miles across the oceans, Tony and Harish were seated in the front seat of Tony's car, Nick and Bryan at the back seat.

TONY: *(To the telephone)* He's here, Boss !

At his Boston North End mansion, Agnitti was getting restless with the delays. "Give him the telephone. *(A pause)* Harish, you stay on the line, your father wants to talk to you from India. *(He pressed a button on the telephone)* Mr. Dixit, this is a three-way connection now, your son is at the other end. Would you like to talk to him ?"

Mr. Dixit's tough Police-Chief facade almost broke down. He talked excitedly to the telephone, "Harish, Harish, Harish, Meyrey Beta (my son), are you all right ... "

In Tony's car, Harish was talking to the car telephone with equal nervousness, "I'm all right, Dad, ... *(Pause)* ... so far no problem ... *(Pause)* ... but, they follow me everywhere ... to my school, to the library, to the gym, everywhere ... *(Pause)* ... what's happened, Dad ? ... why are they doing this, Dad ... are they going to kill me ? ..."

Tears were gathering in Dixit's eyes. "Be careful, Meyrey Beta", he sounded like crying, "it's a foreign country, I don't have any power over there ... *(Pause)* ...no, don't go to police, never even think of going to the police ..."

At this point Mr. Agnitti, who was listening on his third party line, decided to interrupt. "All right, Mr. Dixit. You heard your son. He is safe over here. I kept my part of the promise. Now, you keep your promise. Make sure Nancy is safe. You will get your son back when Nancy comes back to me. She's my only family."

DIXIT: Mr. Agnitti, that was very nice of you. Will you like to talk to Nancy now ?

Dixit gave the telephone to Nancy, "Your uncle wants to talk to you."

Nancy took the telephone.

NANCY: *(To the telephone)* Yes, uncle Vinny, I'm all right ... *(Pause)* ... No, I don't want to go back now ...

I've a lot of unfinished work … *(Pause)* … how can I explain everything over the phone … I'll call you later … *(Pause)* … OK uncle, I do remember you, I love you, … *(Pause)* … yes, I'll go back and I'll be a good little girl again … I promise I'll call you later … *(Pause)* OK …

Nancy gave the telephone to Dixit, "He wants to talk to you."

DIXIT: *(To telephone)* Yes, Mr. Agnitti, Nancy is free to go, I'll see that she is safe in this country, thank you, thank you very much for looking after my son … he is my only son … *(Pause)* …please … please … he is my only son.

Exhausted, Dixit lowered the phone to its cradle. After a pause, Nancy asked …

NANCY: How old is your son, Mr. Dixit ?

DIXIT: Nineteen. Why ?

NANCY: I read a report as to what happened to a seventeen year old boy in your country.

DIXIT: Yes ?

NANCY: This seventeen year-old was the son of a very ordinary family, a peasant family … he knew that Police and Army attacked a neighboring village and raped the womenfolk. So, when police attacked his house, he took his thirty-five year-old mother to the backyard. Both mother and the son were hiding in a foxhole. But, one

133

soldier saw a part of his clothing. They dragged the boy out of the hole, threw him on the ground, stood on his stomach, put the rifle on his temple, and shot him ... right in front of the mother. Her son was seventeen. Your son is nineteen.

DIXIT: *(With panic)* You're not going to tell this to your uncle, are you ?

NANCY: *(Laughed)* How would you feel if somebody with heavy, iron boots stood on your son's stomach and held a rifle on his temple ?

DIXIT: Who told you that story ?

NANCY: I read in Saxena's report.

DIXIT: *(Surprised)* Saxena's report ? That was about Assam. I thought you said something that happened in India.

NANCY: Assam is a part of India, isn't it ?

DIXIT: You don't have to worry about those people. These are ordinary people, uneducated, work in the rice fields, don't have good jobs ... these are not your kind. I'll arrange your itinerary ... you go and stay in the posh hotels in big cities, good food, dances every night, go and see Agra, Simla, Mussouri, Calcutta, Banglore, Bombay, stay in the modern five star hotels, good food ....

NANCY: *(Interrupting)* Good food, dances every night ... thanks, many thanks Mr. Dixit, I do understand I don't have to worry about those ordinary people. Now, if you don't mind, I'd like to go. Do you mind ?

DIXIT: Not at all, let me call your escort ...

Dixit rang the bell. Ashok entered and saluted.

DIXIT: Miss Anderson is free to go. Escort her and get her a taxi.

ASHOK: Yes sir.

Ashok walked to the door and stood outside in the hallway.

NANCY: Thank you, Mr. Dixit.

DIXIT: You're most welcome ! It was nice meeting you ! Please contact me whenever you need anything ...

Nancy went out to the hallway and joined Sneha. "Come on Sneha, let's go. We have lots of things to catch up on."

ASHOK: Sorry, madam, she cannot go.

NANCY: Why not ?

ASHOK: She is under arrest.

NANCY: On what charge ?

ASHOK: *(Read from his notes)* Disorderly conduct.

Nancy flared up in anger. "You scoundrels", she shouted, "you first beat her up and then you charge her with disorderly conduct ?"

In an uncontrollable anger, she gave a loud kick at the door of Mr. Dixit's room. Ashok, Sneha and the two policemen could not believe their own eyes that someone could kick at the door of the Police Chief. Nancy opened the door and walked straight to the desk of Mr. Dixit.

DIXIT: Hello, hello, ... what's the matter ?

NANCY: They don't allow Sneha to go with me.

Dixit tried to scale down the situation by moving his palms up and down, "Don't worry about her ! She is an ordinary girl, I told you, she comes from Mother Ayesha's orphanage, these are very ordinary people ... you don't have to worry about her ... "

Nancy looked straight at the eyes of Mr. Dixit and said slowly, grinding each word separately, "I want that very ordinary girl to go free with me. Is that clear to you ?"

Dixit was smart enough to size up the situation immediately. His attitude and his tone of voice changed accordingly, "Of course she will go with you ! I never knew they arrested her ! *(Called out for the Officer)* Hey

Ashok !"

Ashok entered.

ASHOK: Yes sir !

DIXIT: That girl is free to go with Nancy. Do all the paper work.

ASHOK: All right.

Dixit took out his anger on Ashok. Very angrily, he told him, "Not "all right". Say, "Yes sir". And ... salute !"

"Yes sir !", Ashok saluted and went out, followed by Nancy.

Ashok, Nancy and Sneha, followed by the two constables, walked down the hallway in a formal atmosphere, without saying a word. Ashok stopped in front of a door that had a sign "ASHOK MATRE, I.P.S.". He talked to Nancy and Sneha in the manners of a perfect gentleman.

ASHOK: If you don't mind, I've to do some paperwork and get your signatures.

His manner was so perfect that two girls were visibly impressed. Sneha was the first one to reply ...

SNEHA: That's all right. We understand there are formalities.

137

ASHOK: Will you please come in ?

Inside his office, Ashok got busy with his paper work. Nancy and Sneha were seated in front of him, and watching him. After some time, Nancy asked ...

NANCY: How long is this going to take ?

Ashok raised his head and asked Sneha, "The report says you behaved in a disorderly manner. What really happened ?"

NANCY: She came running and stood between me and those policemen, that's all ! Does the report say that the Officer hit her ?

ASHOK: Hit her ? You said that before ! What was the reason to hit her ?

SNEHA: Is it in the report ?

ASHOK: No !

SNEHA: Are you going to write it down now ?

ASHOK: Yes, of course. You tell me what exactly happened.

SNEHA: How come you're not covering it up ?

NANCY: *(With surprise)* Cover it up ? Why ?

SNEHA: *(To Nancy)* To protect the interest of another

138

police officer !

NANCY: *(To Sneha)* Is that ... kind of ... a common practice over here ?

SNEHA: *(To Nancy)* How long have you been in India ?

Ashok was watching Sneha when Sneha and Nancy were talking. Now he asked, "Sneha, you tell me exactly what happened. I am going to record every word you say. Then, I'll send the report for Departmental Enquiry. Who hit you ? How ?"

Strangely enough, Sneha smiled and shook her head slowly.

SNEHA: I'm not going to answer any of your questions unless you answer mine.

ASHOK: *(With some surprise)* What's your question ?

SNEHA: How come you're not trying to cover the whole thing up ? How come you're so different ? Are you a new recruit ?

ASHOK: *(He smiled, too)* How do you know that Police try to cover up things ?

SNEHA: I used to work for a news magazine. I know everything. Now, answer me, why are you not trying to ...

ASHOK: *(Jokingly)* Are you going to publish my report in your paper ?

SNEHA: *(Jokingly)* Yes ... if your English is good !

ASHOK: *(In mock intimidation)* Do you know they burn down printing presses around here ...

SNEHA: My press is already burnt. You can't burn the ashes !

ASHOK: *(In sudden realization)* Did you work for Sharma ?

SNEHA: Didn't you take a long time to figure that out ?

ASHOK: Now I exactly know why you two are together !

SNEHA: You still didn't answer my question.

ASHOK: *(In mock intimidation)* You don't talk like that to an IPS officer in India !

NANCY: What is the meaning of IPS ? I saw that at the door.

SNEHA: *(To Nancy)* Indian Police Service. *(In mock fear)* It's dangerous !

ASHOK: *(To Sneha, still joking)* You don't seem to be afraid at all !

SNEHA: *(To Ashok, almost affectionately)* How come you're so different ?

ASHOK: Am I ? I wear the same uniform !

SNEHA: *(Entreated him)* Please tell us ! We may not get another chance to see someone like you again ! Nancy will go back to America with an one-sided opinion !

ASHOK: Well, the Department didn't place me here to improve its image for a foreign detainee.

NANCY: *(Jokingly)* Am I a detainee ?

ASHOK: You were, a few minutes back. I'm still wondering how you got around that shark upstairs.

SNEHA: *(Very surprised)* You're calling him a shark ? Sitting in the same building ??

ASHOK: Of course I am ! I'm sick and tired of the political games. The duty of the police department is to uphold law and order. That's how we were trained. We are supposed to arrest even the Prime Minister if she breaks the law.

SNEHA: Does she ?

ASHOK: Why is she trying to impose the illegal electoral roll in Assam ? Isn't it same as breaking the law ?

NANCY: How do you know it is illegal ?

141

ASHOK: There's a non-political judiciary body known as "Election Commission". The Election Commissioner, Mr. Sakhdar, ... he said publicly that the electoral roll of Assam contained millions of illegal names of illegal foreign infiltrators.

NANCY: Oh ! What did the Prime Minister say ?

ASHOK: She said, ... Mr. Sakhdar will retire in July ...

NANCY: What does it mean ?

ASHOK: The elections will be held in February, after Sakhdar retires. Maybe she'll appoint a new Election Commissioner who'll lick her feet ...

SNEHA: *(To Ashok)* I can't believe you're saying this to a foreign tourist. It may cost you your job.

ASHOK: I know. I'm sick and tired of playing the role of a time-server. All my seniors are confirmed time-servers now. For the sake of bread and butter and house and wealth and power and ...

SNEHA: I can't believe I'm hearing this from an IPS officer ...

ASHOK: You know, they hire the most brilliant students into the administrative and police jobs and then make sure that everyone turns into a time-server.

NANCY: You were a brilliant student ?

ASHOK: I was. That's why I passed the tough IPS exam. My older brothers sacrificed everything to give me higher education ...

SNEHA: What about your father ?

ASHOK: He was a great devotee of Mahatma Gandhi. He was a cripple, one leg and one arm broken in a Police beating in the 1942 "Quit India" Movement. He died when I was young. Until his last day, he used to make sure that we boys got up in the morning and dressed properly to attend Independence Day, Republic Day, and other National Events.

SNEHA: So, your brothers raised you ?

ASHOK: All of them sacrificed in order to give me my education. Even some of our neighbors helped out. That's why I feel so obligated. I thought I would serve the country when I get the job. But, can I do my job ? Day before yesterday, the heads of two cows were found in front of a Hindu temple in Amritsar, and, within ten hours, the Prime Minister went to the Parliament and made a statement that the Sikhs had done it. Now rioting is going on between Hindus and Sikhs in Amritsar and a few other cities. How did she know Sikhs did it ? How could she complete a legitimate, judicial enquiry in less than ten hours ? It is possible that the cow-heads were planted by her party workers !

NANCY: That sounds like Watergate !

ASHOK: Watergate Scandal ? Of President Nixon ? Compared to the dirty tricks in Indian politics, Watergate appears like a child's play !

SNEHA: And now, rioting is going on between Sikhs and Hindus ! Innocent people are getting killed ... old, sick, children ...

NANCY: Did she know that her statement would start rioting ?

ASHOK: Of course she knew. Even a school boy would have known that !

SNEHA: *(To Ashok)* However, it is dangerous for you to talk like that.

ASHOK: I know that. I don't know why I'm opening up to you two. Maybe because ours is the same generation. Maybe because you are special in some unknown way.

Nancy and Sneha laughed as if they were much younger and happier.

SNEHA: Maybe because you saw Nancy kick at Dixit's door !

ASHOK: *(Laughed)* Maybe !

SNEHA: But, you mustn't. *(To Nancy)* Do you know he has high price in the dowry market ?

NANCY: I've heard that before. What's this dowry market, anyway ? I was told that an MIT PhD will sell for six hundred thousand rupees in dowry market.

SNEHA: *(With a mischievous smile)* And, an IPS officer will go easily for five hundred thousands !

ASHOK: *(Jokingly)* Nah ! No such luck ! That's the price of IAS Officers !

NANCY: What's that ?

SNEHA: IAS stands for Indian Administrative Service, similar to IPS.

ASHOK: Not in the dowry market ! IAS is much more expensive than IPS in that cattle market of bridegrooms.

NANCY: Cattle market ! My father's uncle was a cattle auctioneer in Texas.

ASHOK: *(Still joking)* Bring him over here ! He'll make big bucks !

SNEHA: Well, an IPS will still sell for four hundred thousands ! *(To Ashok, teasing him)* What will you do when you get four hundred thousand rupees ?

ASHOK: I'll never take that money.

SNEHA: Why ?

ASHOK: I told my brothers. I'll never allow them to take dowry.

NANCY: *(Surprised)* What ?

SNEHA: You can't do that to your brothers ! You said they were poor, they sacrificed everything to give you education.

ASHOK: That doesn't give them the right to sell me in a cattle auction.

SNEHA: Do they agree ?

ASHOK: We are Maharashtrians. We fought with the Islamic rulers for three hundred years. We know how to renunciate. We don't run after material gains like the Delhi-wallas.

NANCY: I don't understand ...

SNEHA: *(To Nancy)* I'll explain to you later.
(To Ashok) But, you're in Delhi now ! Whoever goes to Lanka becomes the Ravana. Will you be able to resist the pressure ?

Ashok's anger was building up. However, he remained calm outside and said slowly, "Damn it ! Somebody has got to break the vicious circle ! I'm going to do everything I can to stop this wicked practice. I've a deal with at least one member of the Parliament who will raise hell in the Parliament if I can give him enough evidence."

NANCY: Are you talking about burning of the brides whose parents fail ...

ASHOK: Yes.

146

NANCY: Why don't you take up the case of Sneha ? Look at her face ! How beautiful she was ! *(Nancy almost cried)* See, what they have done to her face !

All this time, at the back of his mind, Ashok was thinking about Sneha's burn marks. Now, suddenly he could not control his anger. With the full authority of a Police Officer, he demanded, "All right. Give me the names, Sneha. Who did that to you ? I'll go and hang those guys with piano wires."

SNEHA: You can't prove anything in a court of law.

ASHOK: Leave that to me. You give me the names. I was going to ask you right at the beginning. Now, Nancy has spoken for us. Give me the names.

SNEHA: *(Sadly)* No, Ashok ! I don't have any hope in life. I don't have any future. Let me suffer in silence. But, don't you stop ! Go ahead and save another girl who still has some hope, some future, some life !

When they returned from the Police Station, Sneha told Nancy in the taxi, "I think it is pretty late to go to Mother Ayesha's convent at this time."

"What about the Burn Center of Delhi Hospital ?"

"That's late, too."

"Maybe we should get started early in the morning tomorrow", Nancy said.

"That's better ! Where do you want to go first in the morning ?", Sneha asked.

"To the Hospital. I want to talk to the half burnt brides."

"Good idea", Sneha agreed.

"Let me go and drop you at your home", Nancy said. But when she actually arrived Sneha's house, she had a new idea, "Sneha ! Will you let me stay with you tonight ?"

"You ? At my house ?", Sneha was embarrassed, "We're not rich people, Nancy ! We don't have ..."

"It doesn't matter what you don't have ! May I ? Please ?"

"Well, I'll be more than happy ! But, you ... you... what will you wear ?"

Nancy smiled. "I'll have to learn how to wear a sari ! Will you teach me ?"

Both of them laughed like little girls. Nancy paid the taxi driver and accompanied Sneha to her house.

Back in the Meredith Hotel, Jim, Shekhar, Willy and Bob, were making last minute preparations before leaving for the Himalayas.

WILLY: What will be charges of the Sherpa guides ?

SHEKHAR: I don't know. The Nepal Government has made very strict rules about labor payments. We'll know the exact number when we get there.

JIM: Did you hear from Neel ?

SHEKHAR: No ! Did he contact you ?

JIM: He didn't. I hope he will not carry out his threat.

BOB: We should start climbing before Neel changes his mind.

WILLY: Even if he informs the Royal Geographic guys, what harm can they possibly do at this late hour ?

BOB: By the time they put their act together, we'll be at the top of the peak !

SHEKHAR: Right ! But, I thought you said that we'll have to practice before the actual climb.

BOB: Well, we'll be over there tomorrow, we'll start practicing the day after !

SHEKHAR: Tomorrow ! I always run into problems in timing. My father is coming from Moradabad to catch me over here tomorrow.

BOB: Your father ?

SHEKHAR: Yes, my father, the famous Tyagi-ji of Moradabad, I told you guys, he claims to be the right hand man of Indira Gandhi in that area. Somebody told him I'm here, and he sent a message that I should go to see him, I did not, so he's coming himself. Now, if he comes looking for me over here, you guys are going to tell him that I'm not here. I don't want to see him.

JIM: What time is the flight tomorrow ?

WILLY: Ten o' clock.

JIM: We'll get out before he comes. Let's get ready.

SHEKHAR: I must go and leave a message for Nancy.

WILLY: Forget about Nancy, Shekhar ! You've spent plenty of time running after her !

SHEKHAR: I couldn't find her the past two days. We must tell her our whereabouts before we leave, don't you think so ?

On Nancy's part, she was having a very good time in Sneha's house. Sneha taught her how to wear a sari and how to eat Roti (Indian bread) with her fingers. Both of them were giggling at their mistakes. They became very close to each other.

NANCY: When Neel dumped me, I was feeling so helpless ... so angry, so hopeless ... I can't explain ...

SNEHA: Are you still angry ?

NANCY: Yes, of course ! I'm angry at Neel, I'm angry at his bride, I'm angry, I'm angry, I'm just angry ...

SNEHA: Yes, I could see that. Do you always kick the door like that when you're angry ?

NANCY: Oh, today ? Well, *(apologetically)* today was different ! Anybody would be angry at a situation like today's !

SNEHA: But, a girl is not supposed to kick doors like that ...

NANCY: Why not ? If you're genuinely angry, wouldn't you ?

SNEHA: Me ? No ! Oh my God, I couldn't even think of doing that !

NANCY: *(Surprised)* Why not ?

SNEHA: That's against the Code of Laxmi.

NANCY: Laxmi ! I heard that word before. Isn't it the name of a goddess ?

SNEHA: Yes. She's the goddess of ...

NANCY: Goddess of wealth, health, beauty, well-being ...

SNEHA: *(Surprised)* How did you know ?

NANCY: *(With mock pride)* I know a lot of things about Indian culture !

SNEHA: Do you also know about the Code of Laxmi ?

NANCY: No ! What's that ?

SNEHA: All girls are supposed to follow it. According to this Code, a girl mustn't talk loudly, mustn't laugh loudly, mustn't be angry, must be loving and caring to everyone in the family and the neighborhood ...

NANCY: And she mustn't kick down the door of the local Police Chief ?

Both of them burst out laughing.

SNEHA: *(Still laughing)* No, don't joke, these are very serious matters ! Laxmi is the goddess of well-being of the family, well-being of the village ...

NANCY: Village ?

SNEHA: Yes. She has another name, Graamalaxmi, meaning the Laxmi of the village. The other name is Deshalaxmi, the Laxmi of the entire country. The wealth of the country, beauty of the country, the well-being of the country ...

NANCY: So, you follow her code ?

SNEHA: Since I was a little girl ! My mother taught me the Code of Laxmi until her dying day ! Come, I'll show you something ...

Sneha took Nancy by her hand to the next room, which was a prayer room. There was a picture of Goddess Laxmi. Sneha explained to Nancy, "My mother taught me to sing in front of this picture of Goddess Laxmi... why are you looking at the picture like that ? Do you recognize her ?"

Nancy was gazing at the picture of Goddess

Laxmi. There was a striking similarity with the face of Neel's bride, Laxmi. Holding on to her curiosity, Nancy replied, "No ! Just a passing thought. Did you say you pray to Goddess Laxmi for the well-being of the whole country ?"

"Yes, we do, ... why do you ask ?"

"I saw a cultural show the other day at Miranda College. A girl played the role of Mother India over there. I had a passing thought that this picture reminds me of her !"

Sneha replied easily, "That's very natural. For us the Hindus, there is no difference between Goddess Laxmi, or Mother India, or even an individual girl."

"This is something I'll never understand." Nancy's reaction was quick and straightforward. "If they train the girls to acquire the qualities of Goddess Laxmi, why do they burn them over a dowry ?"

Sneha sighed and became quiet. After a pause, she replied softly, "Doctor Sharma has a theory."

"What's that ?", Nancy asked critically.

"Ask him. I'll not be able to explain."

Shekhar tried to finish all his errands and leave for Kathmandu before his father would catch up with him. He went to the "INTERNATIONAL STUDENTS' HOSTEL" to meet Nancy. She was not there. He left a written message with the desk clerk and hurried back to Meredith Hotel.

But, unfortunately, Shekhar did not realize that his father had a large retinue of secret agents of his political party. Spotting Shekhar was an easy task for them. When Shekhar got out of the taxi and was heading towards the hotel, he heard a familiar voice. It was the voice of his father, Tyagi-ji of Moradabad, from behind, "Wait a minute, Shekhar !"

Shekhar turned back. He was very surprised.

SHEKHAR: Father ?

Tyagi was standing besides a long, expensive car.

SHEKHAR: How did you know I was in this hotel ?

TYAGI: Well ...

SHEKHAR: Political tricks, everywhere ...

TYAGI: You must not talk like that to me ! You're my only son !

SHEKHAR: Yeah ? What happened to your only daughter-in-law ?

TYAGI: Shekhar, I must talk to you. You have a lot of misinformation. A lot of misunderstanding. I want to talk to you in privacy. Will you come to my car ?

SHEKHAR: No.

TYAGI: Shekhar, you're the eldest boy of the family, you're the only one to look after your mother and sister ...

SHEKHAR: Mother and sister ! Did you say mother and sister ?

TYAGI: I know you're very angry. I understand that. I would have been just the same if I had the same information. But, your information is all wrong. Will you come inside the car ? I want to show you something !

Shekhar reluctantly accompanied his father to the back seat of the car. The driver was at the front seat, but Tyagi asked him, "Gopal, will you go and stand outside."

"Yes sir."

Gopal, the driver, went out and closed the car door behind him. Tyagi started his pleading defensively, "The information you had was all wrong", he told Shekhar, "Your mother and sister were not responsible for Kamla's death."

SHEKHAR: How do you know ? You were not even home at that time.

TYAGI: *(With some relief)* Yes, I was not home. Had I been home, this would have never happened. I loved Kamla like my own daughter.

SHEKHAR: But, your real daughter did not. And, you took the side of your real daughter.

TYAGI: Shekhar, you're not supposed to talk like that. I'm your father. This is a gross violation of Indian tradition; boys are not supposed to talk back to their parents.

SHEKHAR: And the girls are not supposed to talk loudly, or laugh loudly. They are supposed to be loving and caring for everybody in the family and the neighborhood ...

TYAGI: What is wrong in that ?

SHEKHAR: *(Continuing ...)* ... till one day they're burnt alive.

TYAGI: Don't be so disrespectful. You're my only son. If you leave home, we're all finished. All the money I've made, all the property I've made, these are all for you. In the last two years, I got a few large defence contracts in the ammunition factory in Moradabad, ... we're all set now, I've already saved more than ten million rupees for you, ... ten million ... see what I've got here ...

Tyagi reached for his pocket and took out a key with a tag attached to it. He held it in his palm. The key shined in reflected light. There was a ring with a large diamond on the other side of Tyagi's ring finger. The diamond was so large that its shine was seen even from behind the finger.

Tyagi continued, " ... this is your copy of the key. The name of the Bank and the account number are in the tag. Keep the account number in a separate place."

SHEKHAR: What is it ?

TYAGI: It is the new account I opened in a Swiss Bank. Our box is very near that of Indira Gandhi. So far, I've deposited ten million rupees. Keep the key safely. Try to memorize the account number.

SHEKHAR: If you had so much money, why did you have to kill poor Kamla just for a few hundred thousands ...

Deep down in his stomach, Shekhar felt as if a high-power vacuum pump had sucked up all his existence from within ... a feeling that he had been suffering since the past two and a half years ... a sickness that he managed to forget while he was in the USA ... a sickness that had revived due to the familiar environment in India. He covered his face with his two palms and went on babbling in a choked voice ..... "she was so nice, she took care of everybody, she gave love to everybody, humming songs while doing her housework, she was smiling and loving and caring to everyone ..."

TYAGI: Don't cry Shekhar ! I cried when I got the news. We can't bring her back by crying. Life goes on. Let's make the best out of whatever is left. You are my only son. I want to make you happy. That's why I convinced the Party Boss to give me these defence contracts. Now we have all the money that we need. Keep the key. Keep the account number.

SHEKHAR: I don't want your money.

TYAGI: You're still angry. Don't be angry. It is a lot of money.

SHEKHAR: You're showing money to me ? Why did my mother and sister ...

TYAGI: Your mother and sister were not responsible for Kamla's death, I told you. Wait a minute. I'll show you a copy of Kamla's dying statement at the Police Station ...

He kept the key in his pocket and took out a paper.

TYAGI: *(Continued ...)* Read this. This is a copy of the statement she gave at the police station just before she died. It says clearly she overturned the kerosene stove, which burst into flame ... read it, read it, read it yourself

159

...

Shekhar eyed the paper and became very grave.

SHEKHAR: All right. I've to go to Nepal tomorrow. When I come back, I'll talk to mother and sister ...

TYAGI: *(Overjoyed)* Your sister is in her husband's home now ! I paid all the balance of her dowry money. She'll come home to see you as soon as you come ...

Shekhar opened the door and got out of the car.

TYAGI: When will you return from Nepal ?

SHEKHAR: Very soon.

TYAGI: *(Happily)* That's good, that's good, that's very good ...

Shekhar was going, but he turned back, put his head in the car window, and asked in a sharp, pointed voice ...

SHEKHAR: How much did you pay for that Police Report, father ?

TYAGI: *(Taken aback)* You mean the Dying Statement ?

SHEKHAR: Will you go and take your money back from those guys at the Police Station ? They didn't do a good job for you. Ask them, if Kamla died in a kerosene stove accident in the kitchen in our house, why ... why did she run half a mile to the Police Station to give that Dying Statement ?

Tyagi was dumbfounded.

SHEKHAR: I saw the real Dying Statement. The day after. At the Police Station. The one you have is a fake, like your entire life is a fake ...

Shekhar walked up the steps of Meredith Hotel. The long car of Tyagi remained motionless for a long time.

Next morning, Shekhar, Jim, Bob and Willy flew to Kathmandu. Jim, Bob and Willy were excited when they saw the panoramic view of the Himalayan Mountain Range above the cloud level. The sky was very blue.

BOB: Look at the Himalayas ! Look at the Himalayas !

JIM: Ah ! That's magnificent !

WILLY: Didn't I tell you ! It's worth the trip !

Shekhar went on looking at the deep blue sky, without a word, without a smile.

Back in New Delhi, Phulraj was busy in his daily chores. He came out with a fat file from a room marked "PHULRAJ MATHUR, PRIVATE SECRETARY TO PRIME MINISTER" and entered a room marked "PRIME MINISTER", in the South Block of the huge Secretariat Building of India.

In the surrealistic ambience of the Prime Minister's office, Phulraj Mathur appeared to be much less than his actual size. He was standing in front of a long conference table. A picture of Mahatma Gandhi was hanging on the wall on one side.

PHULRAJ: The Assam boys have been waiting since morning, Memsahib !

The voice of Indira Gandhi appeared to have reverberated from a great distance, "Let them wait. The Prime Minister of India is not so easily available."

PHULRAJ: *(Beaming with great appreciation)* I like it ! I like it ! That's exactly what Nehru-ji said to that Naga delegation years ago. Ha ha !

VOICE OF INDIRA GANDHI: Don't patronize me, Phulraj !

PHULRAJ: *(His smile turned into a regret)* I'm very sorry, madam, I'm very sorry, madam !

VOICE OF INDIRA GANDHI: Go and bring them.

"Yes, madam ! Thank you, madam !"

Phulraj went out and came back with the Assam delegation. They looked tired and bored. They took their seats around the long conference table, looking up at the high platform of Indira Gandhi. They all appeared to be much less than their actual size.

GOGOI: We do understand you have a difficult task to do. But, it was not our fault. Protection of the international border was the duty of Government of India. The foreigners just walked across the border. The Government of India failed to stop them. The foreigners have overrun our home and hearth. It is like a civilian invasion ...

VOICE OF INDIRA GANDHI: Don't exaggerate. There are illegal immigrations across borders all over the world. Look at the border between Texas and Mexico in the USA ...

GOGOI: That's a good analogy because the population of Assam is almost same as that of Texas. Just imagine what the Texans would do if four million Mexicans, forty per cent of the total population of Texas, cross the border and overran them !

VOICE OF INDIRA GANDHI: That's an exaggerated number. Every country in the world has illegal immigrants ...

GOGOI: Forgive me, Madam, the phrase "illegal immigrant" cannot be used in our discussion because it is an oxymoron like "dark sunlight". It doesn't make any sense. The word "immigrant" means those people who enter another country with some passport, some kind of a visa, some kind of documents. These foreigners do not have any passport, they don't have any visa, they don't have any document whatsoever. They just walked in across the border. They are "illegal infiltrators". They are not "illegal immigrants".

VOICE OF INDIRA GANDHI: You shouldn't worry about them. I'm giving you a grant of one hundred millions rupees for development works in Assam. That'll be plenty of money for all of you.

GOGOI: We don't want any money. We want our land back. Since 1951, the Government of India had been giving assurances to the people of Assam that the infiltrators would be detected and deported. Please see these newspaper clippings ... *(He dumped a large number of news paper clippings, clipped serially by date, on the table)* ... these are the clippings of local newspapers since 1951, each reporting either the infiltration of Pakistani nationals or the promise of the Government of India to deport them. Our fault was that we believed in the Government of India. Since 1951, they went on giving promises whenever we complained, but they did not take any action to keep their promise. They deceived us. This amounts to betrayal.

VOICE OF INDIRA GANDHI: You are talking very well. Who is giving you training you talk like this ? Who is your leader ?

Gogoi pointed to the picture of Mahatma Gandhi, and stated conclusively, "He is our leader."

Indira Gandhi did not expect this. She always dubbed the Assam Movement as unpatriotic. She wanted the whole world to believe that the Assamese people were anti-national and violent. Her propaganda would now look silly if the agitators pointed to Mahatma Gandhi, the apostle of nonviolent struggle against injustice, as their leader. She was shaken up, but controlled the situation very quickly ...

VOICE OF INDIRA GANDHI: If he is your leader, why don't you listen to him ? He always preached love and affection. You should give love and affection to the poor people of Bangladesh who infiltrated into your land to save their lives from the famine and hunger in their own country.

GOGOI: If saving life from famine and hunger is their main concern, why are they so anxious to enter their names into the electoral rolls ? If they are so poor, where are they getting money to bribe the unscrupulous election officials and enter their names into the electoral rolls ? The electoral rolls of Assam contain millions of names of foreigners. This will deprive the democratic rights of genuine citizens. This is gross injustice. After complaining for twenty-eight years, we launched a peaceful non-violent demonstration, following the path of Mahatma Gandhi. The Government of India opened fire on peaceful demonstrators. The Indian Army attacked our houses and raped our mothers and sisters. You did not take any step to punish the guilty. This is a vilest act of defiling the Deshalaxmi, and you covered it up by false and fake reports.

At the front desk of Delhi Hospital, Nancy was enquiring her way in the Burn Center, "Which way is the female ward of the Burn Center ?"

Sneha pulled Nancy from behind, "Come on, I know the way ! "

Most of the patients at the female ward of the Burn Center were young girls. Some of the patients had their heads wrapped. Nurses were walking around. Nancy and Sneha approached one patient whose head was not wrapped.

SNEHA: *(To the patient)* How are you, dear ?

PATIENT: Much better now. Who are you ?

SNEHA: I used to work for Mother Ayesha. This is Nancy. What's your name ?

PATIENT: Rami. Yours ?

SNEHA: I'm Sneha. What happened, Rami ?

RAMI: The house caught fire. We didn't know. We all got out, then I realized little Munna was left inside.

Rami covered her face with her two palms.

NANCY: Could you bring the baby out ?

Rami nodded.

RAMI: One beam fell on my side. My husband pulled me out ?

NANCY: Is Munna all right ?

Rami smiled. She thanked heavens by saluting upwards.

RAMI: Goddess Chandi saved my little baby !

SNEHA: Where was your mother-in-law ? Did she come out to help ?

RAMI: My mother-in-law ? She is in the village home. My husband and myself and the baby ... we live in the town ...

Nancy and Sneha were back in the aisle, walking in between Nurses and patients. "That was not a dowry burning !", Nancy whispered to Sneha.

SNEHA: No. But, you'll run into those very soon.

The next patient they interviewed had a bandage around her head, but she could talk. Her name, she said, was Roopa.

ROOPA: No. I told you. It was a pure accident.

NANCY: You're trying to protect somebody ...

SNEHA: We're not going to give your name out.

ROOPA: *(Smiled)* I know what you mean. There are a few cases like that. You see that girl *(pointed to a patient three beds down in the row)* ... I think you should find out about her ...

Nancy and Sneha moved to that patient. She had bandages all over her body, except the head. She was unconscious. Nancy and Sneha tried to talk to her. She did not respond. Sneha ran her fingers through the hair of the girl and smelled the oil.

SNEHA: Oh my God !

NANCY: What is it ?

Nancy ran her fingers through the hair of the girl and smelled.

SNEHA: That's the smell of kerosene oil.

Back in the aisle, Nancy whispered to Sneha, "I

heard what they said about kerosene oil in that CBS report."

SNEHA: It's a petroleum product. Used as fuel in stoves. Easily available in the market.

The next patient they talked was very agitated. Her name was Abha.

ABHA: No. Please go away. They'll kill me if they see me talking to you.

NANCY: Why ?

ABHA: Some newspaper girl was here before ! I told her it was an accident. The stove burst ... and my sari caught fire ...

SNEHA: Are you sure it was the stove ?

The patient from the next bed, Manu, spoke up. Nancy and Sneha looked at her.

MANU: Abha, tell them the truth. We don't have to be afraid any more.

NANCY: I'm Nancy. What's your name ?

MANU: I'm Manu. You know, my husband ... my own husband poured kerosene oil on me ...

She covered her face with her hand and cried.

ABHA: You said you wouldn't cry any more.

170

MANU: We are newly married. I loved him so much ... *(she said in between her sobs.)*

Sneha went to Manu and held her. Nancy was silent. There was fire in her eyes.

NANCY: *(To Abha, slowly)* And, who did this to you ?

ABHA: My mother-in-law, and her servant. My husband was not home.

By this time, Shyama, the matronly head nurse, accompanied by two other nurses, arrived there to enquire about Nancy and Sneha.

SHYAMA: What are you doing here ?

SNEHA: I used to work for Mother Ayesha. How's she *(meaning the patient)* doing ?

SHYAMA: Who is she ? *(meaning Nancy.)*

SNEHA: She's a friend of mine.

SHYAMA: I hope she is not from any newspaper or some foreign television company !

NANCY: No ! Not at all ! Why are you so afraid of the newspapers and foreign television companies ?

SHYAMA: They go out and give all bad publicity about our country. That's why Asthana Sahib told us not to allow ...

171

NANCY: *(Sternly)* May I talk to your Asthana Sahib ?

SHYAMA: Yes. In fact he asked me to call you to his office.

Nancy and Sneha were escorted through the row of beds. On their way, they met Dr. Seeta Kalra, a lady doctor of the same age as Sneha.

SEETA: *(To Sneha)* Sneha ?

SNEHA: How are you Seeta ? *(To Nancy)* This is Doctor Seeta Kalra, I told you about her … we went to the same high school. *(To Seeta)* Seeta, this is Nancy. She is from America.

SEETA: *(To Nancy)* Hi, how are you ?

SHYAMA: I have orders from Doctor Asthana to take them to his office.

SEETA: Oh ! All right, Sneha, Nancy, I'll meet you later.

Nancy and Sneha walked through the rows of beds, escorted by Shyama. They met Dr. Asthana at his office. He was a middle-aged man in doctor's uniform. Nancy and Sneha were ushered in. Dr. Asthana greeted them, requested them to take seats, and asked Shyama to leave.

ASTHANA: I got a report that you were interviewing the patients. Are you from any newspaper or some foreign TV ?

NANCY: I've heard that question before. Why are you so afraid of foreign TV ?

ASTHANA: We're not afraid ! These foreign TV people always misrepresent India ! They don't understand anything.

NANCY: What is there to understand ? Half of your female patients are newly married girls burnt by their in-laws because of dowry disputes ...

ASTHANA: It's not true.

NANCY: Doctor Asthana, you're a middle-aged man. Do you have a daughter ?

ASTHANA: Yes, I do, but ...

NANCY: How would you feel if your daughter was burnt alive ?

ASTHANA: *(Excitedly)* That cannot happen ! I've saved up enough money for her dowry ! I'll pay her dowry in advance !! I'll never keep any dowry balance outstanding.

NANCY: *(A pause)* So, you don't blame the in-laws who burnt these girls !

ASTHANA: I have sympathy for these girls. As a doctor,

I do my best to give medical treatment to these girls. But, ... you must understand ... if the parents of these girls fail to pay the money ... the parents should be more careful ... they shouldn't get into an agreement that they cannot keep ...

After some more discussion that went in circles, Sneha and Nancy came out from Dr. Asthana's office. Nancy closed the door behind her with an audible bang. They met Dr. Seeta in the hallway.

SEETA: Will you come to my office, please ! I want to talk to you both.

Inside her office, Seeta tried to explain, "How can I blame Dr. Asthana when I myself thought like that for a long time ? *(To Sneha)* Remember, I refused to give you the information for your newspaper ?"

NANCY: Have you since changed your mind ?

SEETA: Yes. When I saw the suffering of those girls ... day in ... day out ... months after months ... I broke down. I started to collect the data. In fact, *(To Sneha)* I was going to contact you any way ...

SNEHA: Where are those records ?

Seeta reached for her drawers, fished out a file, gave it to Nancy and said, "Here it is. There are more than three hundred cases in this file. Half of these girls are dead."

Nancy gasped, "Oh my God!"

"These are only a few cases." Seeta went on explaining, "There are many more. I couldn't get all the records. There a few survivors. Most of them are picked up by their relatives. We call Mother Ayesha to take those girls who don't have a place to go."

SNEHA: *(Smiled)* Like me!

NANCY: *(To Seeta)* Tell me one thing. Are all these dowry victims newly married?

SEETA: Not necessarily. Tell her about Apu and his mother, Sneha!

NANCY: Who is Apu?

SNEHA: He is a five year old orphan in Mother Ayesha's convent. You'll see him when you come there.

NANCY: What about him?

SNEHA: Apu was a very talkative four year old boy when they burnt his mother.

NANCY: Oh my God!

SEETA: His mother's name was Asha, meaning "Hope".

SNEHA: When her baby was born, Asha had a hope that the in-laws will forgive her and forget her dowry balance.

NANCY: But, they didn't ?

SNEHA: No. They needed the money. The only way to get money was to marry again. But, they couldn't do that if Asha was alive.

NANCY: Oh my God !

SEETA: They didn't have enough money even to bribe the Police. So, ... after Asha was burnt ... Police arrested them. They are all in jail now.   NANCY: They means who ?

SNEHA: Husband. Mother-in-law. The boy was adopted by Mother Ayesha.

SEETA: They even forgot to hide it from the child. The boy saw everything. He saw them pouring the kerosene oil. He saw them throwing the lighted matches. He saw his mother bursting into flames.

NANCY: And, he was only four ? He saw everything ? What happened to him ?

SNEHA: You'll see it for yourself.

On their way out from the hospital, Nancy told Sneha, "I had an impression that you Hindus are very spiritual people !"

Outside of the hospital, Sneha spotted the white van of Mother Ayesha. Mother Ayesha was not in the van. She had gone inside to pick up another patient. Sneha and Nancy waited till Mother Ayesha came out from the hospital. She was a middle-aged nun, with an innocent, childlike face that radiated transparent holiness. She was escorting a girl patient to her van, assisted by the driver of the van. Sneha came running to her. Mother Ayesha beamed when she saw Sneha.

SNEHA: Mother Ayesha !

AYESHA: Sneha ! My daughter !

SNEHA: Mother, see, whom *(meaning Nancy)* I have here with me ! *(To Nancy)* Nancy, this is Mother Ayesha I told you about !

NANCY: Mother, we had a plan to come and see you at your convent.

AYESHA: In fact, you may come with me right now ! See, we have a new gem for our Convent today *(meaning the patient she picked up)*. She is Kunti. Would you like to come up and sit down with her ?

SNEHA: Mother, Nancy wants to see Apu.

AYESHA: Apu ? Oh, there's good news about Apu. He has started to speak one or two words.

Sneha and Nancy got into the van. The van left the hospital.

Shekhar's father, Mr. Tyagi, had to attend a few party meetings before returning to Moradabad. One such secret meeting was held in the house of Phulraj Mathur in New Delhi, attended by Yashpal, Makkhanlal and Tyagi.

PHULRAJ: So, Makkhanlal, you failed again ! Why was it so difficult to continue a simple Hindu-Sikh rioting just for a few more days ?

MAKKHANLAL: It was not my fault. The opposition papers started the question "Why is the Prime Minister blaming the Sikhs for the cow-heads in front of the Hindu temple ? How ... how did she know that it was done by the Sikhs ? Every Sikh respects a cow just like a Hindu ! How did she know ? Did she order a regular judicial enquiry ? How did she complete the judicial enquiry in less than twelve hours ? Why did she make a statement in the parliament in less than twelve hours ? Just to incite the Hindus ? " All that kind of thing.

PHULRAJ: We all know that. According to our plan, she was supposed to give the statement after three days. I didn't even know that she was going to speak that very night in the Parliament. Yashpal-ji, you're a Member of the Parliament, that was your department !

YASHPAL: *(Defensively)* What could I do ? She did not even tell me ! She just went there and ...

TYAGI: There's no point blaming her. She is under great pressure. We're her assistants. If we don't understand her, what do you expect from the opposition parties ?

PHULRAJ: Tyagi-ji is right. *(To Tyagi)* That's why she likes you most. She told me to put the Assam problem completely in your hands.

TYAGI: I have some ideas about that.

MAKKHANLAL: What's that ?

PHULRAJ: Let's first handle the Sikh problem, then we'll go to the Assam problem. Oh, by the way, *(To Yashpal)* Yashpal-ji, she told me to tell you to make a speech in the Parliament saying that with so many problems in the country, the opposition will never be able to run the country. The country needs a stable government, and only the Nehru family can give a stable government in India, like her father Jawaharlal Nehru who gave a stable government ...

YASHPAL: She told me that before, and I wrote the speech. But, people are laughing at me because I'm the only Member of Parliament giving the same speech again and again ! You should find somebody else ...

PHULRAJ: We all know that, but the Members of Parliament are getting very expensive these days, you know, you have to spend almost one million rupees to buy a Member of Parliament in today's market.

MAKKHANLAL: I can get one at much less price.

PHULRAJ: How much ?

MAKKHANLAL: About six hundred thousand. You'll save four hundred thousand ...

PHULRAJ: And you will ask for half of the savings as your commission ! No, Makkhanlal-ji, I don't think she'll agree, she's particularly unhappy with you, after you refused to do so many things because you're a Brahmin.

TYAGI: I'm a Brahmin, too, but I don't refuse to do anything for her. To serve her is like serving the country. What happened to that slogan "Indira is India" ?

MAKKHANLAL: *(Protesting)* I was the first one to coin that slogan, and nobody would even give me any credit !

YASHPAL: Anyway, what do you want to do about the Sikh problem now ?

PHULRAJ: Well, the two cow-heads started the Hindu Sikh rioting, but it stopped because of that damned propaganda of the opposition parties. Now, we've got to start the rioting up again and then we will be able to send the military to crush the Sikhs.

TYAGI: What about Bhinderwala ?

PHULRAJ: He's our only hope at this time. He is a very good Sikh leader. He is upset because the Hindus killed a few Sikhs at the beginning of the riots. Hopefully, he will now kill some Hindus, and then we will be able to send the Army to crush the Sikhs.

MAKKHANLAL: That's wonderful ! You crush the Sikhs and get the Hindu votes at one stroke. What is the plan about the Assam problem ?

PHULRAJ: We're depending upon Tyagi-ji about that.

TYAGI: Well, thirty million rupees have all been spent to organize the tribals against the Assam Movement.

YASHPAL: You want more money ?

TYAGI: Of course ! Do you know the prices of the things these days ? Particularly when you've to train the tribesmen to use automatic submachine guns ?

PHULRAJ: How's the training going ?

TYAGI: Not good. The tribesmen are excellent in bows and arrows, but, these modern submachine guns ? These are very new for them.

MAKKHANLAL: That must be the reason why most of the casualties result in just injuries, not deaths.

PHULRAJ: That's not acceptable. You can't arouse public sentiment only with small injuries.

TYAGI: There's one basic problem. The tribals are expert in bows and arrows. Their arrows are poisoned. That's why they don't have to worry about aiming very well. If the arrow touches any part of the body, the man will be killed by the poison.

YASHPAL: So, you have to train them more in target practice.

TYAGI: No. Give them poison bullets ! That solves the problem.

MAKKHANLAL: Poison bullets ?

YASHPAL: Where will you get poison bullets ?

Tyagi took out a sample from his pocket and showed it proudly ...

TYAGI: I'm a defence contractor ! I know what to do !

Everybody looked at Tyagi's palm. In addition to the diamond ring on the finger, there was a bullet on his palm.

TYAGI: This is the poison bullet I was talking about ! Look, there's a small capillary hole there. This hole will be filled with a deadly poison. When the bullet hits the man, the poison will get into his blood stream.

MAKKHANLAL: That's a marvelous idea.

YASHPAL: Does she know this ?

PHULRAJ: I don't think we need to tell her. If the tribals kill a lot of Assamese, their agitation will break down and she will be happy. She need not have to know how that happened ! *(To Tyagi)* When are you going to start this ?

TYAGI: We can issue these as soon as you give the approval ...

Mother Ayesha's Convent was a small shrine at the bank of the Yamuna river. The lot was landscaped with trees and grass. There were a few small buildings. It was spring time. Birds and squirrels were playing in the trees. Some children were playing in the yard. When Nancy arrived at the convent, she immediately remembered something that she loved best: the Peace Corps Work in Mexico ! Without wasting any time, she started to work with the other volunteers, as if she had been there for a long time !

Sneha came to her and quipped, "No one would know it is your first day here !"

"I've done this work many times before !", Nancy replied while helping a volunteer to feed an invalid girl.

"Come on, it is your lunch break now !", Sneha said affectionately, "Mother sent me to call you."

At lunch, Ayesha tried her best to answer the barrage of Nancy's questions.

AYESHA: No. That's not true. I was never officially converted to Christianity. I was born as a Muslim. I am still a Muslim. But, the education I had in England opened my eyes.

NANCY: I'm told that most of the Arab girls who get education in England or America don't want to go back to Arabia.

AYESHA: That's true. In my case, I went back to Arabia, and tried to change the things.

SNEHA: What things ?

AYESHA: Islam is very cruel to women.

NANCY: What do you mean ?

AYESHA: In Islam, a man can have four wives, and he can divorce any one of them at any time. But, the wife does not have any rights.

SNEHA: But, I'm told, the husband must pay compensation if he divorces his wife.

AYESHA: Theoretically, yes. But in practice, the woman is the weak party. She may not have attorney's fees to force the husband to pay the compensation.

NANCY: And, the husband can divorce, but the wife cannot ?

AYESHA: That's true. And when that happens, the wife doesn't have any rights excepting that compensation. As for money and property, husband owns everything, wife owns nothing. And the property includes the children. The children of a divorced woman live with the father.

Nancy was surprised. "Oh my God !", she exclaimed.

AYESHA: There are many more injustices to women. Women must cover their bodies, from toe to head, in a black dress, even in the hottest summer day. The religious police will patrol the streets and if they see even an ankle of a woman, she will be dragged to a magistrate for punishment.

NANCY: Oh my God ! Why do you keep on tolerating this ?

SNEHA: I'm told women are not allowed to drive a car in Saudi Arabia ?

AYESHA: That's correct ! I was the niece of a Sheik, and even I couldn't ! You should read the book "Dagger of Islam" to understand what they do to women under Islam. I tried to organize a non-violent protest in the same line as Martin Luther King or Mahatma Gandhi. The same thing happened in another Muslim country, Pakistan.

NANCY: What happened in Pakistan ?

AYESHA: The Pakistani women staged a non-violent protest on the issue of injustice to women. The Army attacked them and crushed them. A similar thing happened in Iran.

SNEHA: What about your country, Saudi Arabia ?

AYESHA: In my country, I couldn't even start anything. So I left my country. I came to India, hoping that since this is the land of Mahatma Gandhi, I'll be able to launch a non-violent fight against injustice ...

NANCY: What did you find ?

AYESHA: Something that I'll never understand. So, I opened this convent for homeless women and their children ... I asked my uncle, the Sheikh, to send a donation ...

NANCY: Did he ?

AYESHA: No.

NANCY: Why not ?

AYESHA: He asked me if these homeless women were Muslim.

NANCY: What did you say ?

AYESHA: I replied, some of them were Muslim, but mostly these were half-burnt Hindu brides ... and he said no.

NANCY: Why not ?

AYESHA: He would give donations only if they were Muslim, or, only if they converted to Islam ...

188

NANCY: So ?

AYESHA: Well, I got donations from some Christian, Jewish and Hindu organizations. Even my uncle is reconsidering his position now ... well, in this kind of work, you're not supposed to give up ... people will change and come back to help you ...

After lunch, Ayesha took them to Apu's room in the Children's Ward. Nancy immediately fell in love with little Apu. He was such a sweet little boy ! Nancy held him to her bosom, gave him some candies and tried to talk to him. Apu didn't reply a word.

SNEHA: Apu does not talk any more, Nancy !

Nancy released Apu. He went back to his desk. He went on looking at Nancy and drew something on the paper with his crayons, while the ladies were talking about him.

AYESHA: He has improved a little bit. Yesterday, he said two words.

SNEHA: Did he ? What did he say ?

AYESHA: It was not clear. But, he tried. I think he tried to say "Nehi".

NANCY: What's the meaning of that ?

SNEHA: That means "Don't".

Nancy looked at Apu. Apu smiled and tried to hide what he was drawing.

NANCY: Let me see what you're drawing !

Nancy went over to Apu's desk and said, "Look, he is drawing me !"

Ayesha and Sneha came over to see Apu's drawing.

SNEHA: *(To Nancy)* See, he colored the skirt green, like yours. The blouse is little more yellow, though !

AYESHA: That's all he does ! He does not speak a word, but he keeps on drawing. I have a box full of his drawings.

Suddenly, Apu took the drawing and ran to the corner of the room. He threw the drawing on the floor, started to smear it with a red crayon, all around the figure that he drew. Sneha ran after him and tried to stop him. Apu started to cry inconsolably.

NANCY: *(To Ayesha)* What happened ?

SNEHA: This happened before.

NANCY: What ?

SNEHA: He drew me one day like that. Then he smeared it with red crayon and cried.

AYESHA: The red crayon is the fire in his mind's eye. He is crying because his mother is on fire.

Later in the taxi, Nancy did not say a single word. After talking alone for a while, Sneha gave up. "You have become like Apu", she said.

"To the last day of my life, I'll not forget what I saw today", Nancy's voice was very heavy.

SNEHA: What are you going to do about it ?

NANCY: I'll come back to Apu. Let me go and finish my work first.

SNEHA: Like what ?

NANCY: Will you take me to some of your Hindu rituals, and make me understand, like wedding, Godbhari, …

Sneha laughed at Nancy's accent, "Godbhari ? Where did you pick up those tough, tough words ?"

Nancy smiled weakly. "Didn't I say it right ? You must take me to those rituals and explain everything."

Sneha tried her best to lighten Nancy's mind. "All right, I'll do that ! But, you must promise to keep your temper down and not to kick anything again !"

Both of them laughed heartily.

When Tyagi arrived at Moradabad after his New delhi trip, he was confronted by his wife, Amba.

AMBA: Why did he not come with you ?

TYAGI: He won't come home. He is adamant.

AMBA: Did you tell him about me ?

TYAGI: I did.

AMBA: He doesn't care for his own mother ! Did you tell him about the money ?

TYAGI: He refused. Didn't even touch the key.

Amba started to cry. She knew, instinctively, that she would have to follow the law of creation: reap what you sow.

AMBA: I'm never going to see my son again ! Why, why is he so obstinate ? Thousands of brides are burnt every year, nobody bothers ! Why ... why has he got to be so different ?

TYAGI: He said he would come back very soon from Nepal. But, his tone was not good. I think he was lying to me.

AMBA: I'm very much afraid. I don't want to lose him forever. Let's do a prayer to Goddess Bhabani. May be She'll change his mind.

TYAGI: That's a good idea. I'll send for the Brahmin priest to do the prayer. Shekhar will definitely come back to you. You take some rest now !

A Brahmin Priest came to their house and performed a Pooja (prayer) to Eternal Mother. The Priest chanted from the sacred books. Amba and Tyagi attended respectfully. Amba could not concentrate on the prayers. She kept on thinking about Shekhar.

At Kathmandu Air Port, Shekhar, Jim, Willy and Bob were busy taking delivery of their supplies, hiring a taxi and loading and travelling. They arrived the Kathmandu International Hotel. They were busy making telephone calls, riding in the taxi, holding an interview with Sherpa laborers, going to government offices, etc.

In spite of all the mountaineering activities, Shekhar couldn't cast aside the memories of Kamla that returned to him due to the familiarity of the surroundings. In his hotel room, there was a wide window, overlooking a magnificent view of the Himalayan Mountains. Shekhar had had many sleepless nights, like this one, looking at the mountain range in the moonlight, all alone. When the morning came, he went out to walk in the garden behind the hotel. It was Spring. Varieties of birds were playing in the garden. Shekhar tried to spot a few humming birds, Kamla's favorite. He remembered how Kamla was running after humming birds in that garden on their honeymoon, laughing, dragging Shekhar with her, laughing again. She would like to turn into a humming bird, she said. Maybe, she really turned into one. Maybe, she was one of those humming birds today. Shekhar went on staring at the humming bird till its image got blurred.

Sneha and Nancy attended a few wedding ceremonies and rituals in Delhi area. Nancy was trying her best to understand the rituals and the customs. She still had the invitation to Neel's wedding. And she still had the gun in her purse ! She had some strange feelings in her mind, which she herself could not understand any more.

Sneha didn't know that Nancy had a gun. However, she came to learn about Nancy's frustration over Neel's wedding. Nancy had a hard time to convince Sneha to accompany her to Neel's "Godbhari".

SNEHA: So, this is the bride's house ?

NANCY: Yes. And remember, this is not the wedding. Today is the Godbhari. Did I say it right this time ?

SNEHA: Are you sure you want to go in ?

NANCY: *(Smiled at Sneha's concern)* Are you still worrying about my temper ?

The house was joyfully decorated. The wedding music was going on in the background. A large gathering of people were moving around busily. Women were in brilliant silk saris. Neel was not there. The bridegroom was not supposed to come to the Godbhari. Neel's mother and sister, Tara and Reena, saw Nancy and were very much concerned. They went to Makkhanlal and confided something in whispers. Nancy coolly approached them and said her greetings very calmly. She talked easily, removing the apprehension of Neel's family.

The ritual began. Laxmi, the bride, dressed in a magnificent silk sari, with gold embroidery all over, was escorted to a small dais at the center of the room. A Brahmin Priest recited some scripts monotonously. Tara gave silk and gold to the bride. She then took out a one hundred rupee currency note, circled her hand three times around the head of the bride and gave the money to the bride. Others repeated the same ritual, everyone swinging currency notes around the bride's head. The Brahmin priest continued to recite the script monotonously.

Nancy and Sneha were seated at the end of the room. "Why do they circle the currency notes around her head ?"

"Do you think it doesn't look good ?" Sneha did not understand what was wrong in that.

The ritual continued. The segment with the currency notes had come to an end. Now the Brahmin Priest announced, "The Godbhari is now completed. Now, gentlemen, you should talk about the give and take and finalize the dowry transactions ... "

When Sneha translated that to Nancy, she could not believe it ! She asked Sneha, "Is that what the Priest said ? Is it included in your scriptures ?"

"I don't know !", Sneha replied.

"Are they going to talk about money deals right here in the public ?"

"That's very common !"

Next, they went to another ritual in a family known to Sneha. This time, the bride-groom was seated on a dais.

SNEHA: *(To Nancy)* This is called the "Tilak", in which the bride-groom is congratulated.

NANCY: Will they talk about money here too ?

SNEHA: I never thought there was anything wrong. Now I can see how you're looking at it.

The ritual began. A Brahmin Priest recited some scripts monotonously. A middle-aged man, apparently the father of the bride, gave silk and gold to the bride-groom and decorated his forehead with sandal paste. He then took out a one hundred rupee currency note, circled it three times around the head of the groom, and gave the money to him. Others repeated the same ritual with currency notes. One elderly lady put a garland made of currency notes, around the neck of the groom. The Brahmin priest kept on reciting the holy script monotonously, and said at the end, as if it was a part of the script, "The Tilak is now completed. Now, gentlemen, you should talk about the give and take, the dowry transactions ..."

Nancy was holding her breath when she saw the events in the next few minutes. "Oh My God, what's going on ? Are they fighting over dowry ?"

SNEHA: That's not very common ! Most of the people settle these matters in private.

The father of the groom was yelling at the father of the bride, who was listening with his head down.

Nancy did not understand everything. "What's going on ?", she asked Sneha.

Sneha whispered, "There is a dispute over the final figure. The father of the groom is accusing the father of the bride of cheating and undercutting ..."

"What'll happen now ?"

"The others are intervening. I think they'll find out a number acceptable to both sides."

"It is like a fish market !"

Nancy and Sneha attended, at Nancy's insistence, more wedding rituals and weddings for the next few weeks for other couples. The rituals were same, showing the varying degree of money deals, inspections of jewelry and other extortions, quarrels, break-downs and reconciliations.

"I have collected so much data", Nancy confided to Sneha, "that I'll have to change the subject of my research project !"

In the process, Nancy also attended the final wedding of her ex-fiance, Neel. She saw that the groom and bride went around the fire seven times, while their fathers were still arguing over the dowry at another part of the wedding canvas.

When Nancy and Sneha arrived Sneha's house in a taxi, they found a police jeep in front of the house where Ashok was waiting in full Police Uniform.

ASHOK: I was about to leave. Where did you two go ?

NANCY: *(Laughing)* We're back from an expedition !

SNEHA: *(Jokingly)* Are you coming to invite us to the Police Station again ?

ASHOK: *(Laughing)* No, I have something to show you. May I come in ?

SNEHA: Oh, sure !

Inside Sneha's house, sitting on wooden chairs, sipping tea, Ashok came to the serious subject very quickly.

ASHOK: I found the address of Doctor Sharma. He is in Kathmandu.

SNEHA: *(Excitedly)* Oh my God ! How did you find it ?

ASHOK: *(Teasing her)* You think we Police Officers are good for nothing, don't you ?

NANCY: That's great ! All my friends are in Kathmandu. I'll be able to contact him there.

ASHOK: Your friends ?

NANCY: Yes. They came to climb a Himalayan peak. In fact, I'm a member of their team.

ASHOK: Please remember, this information is very secret.

SNEHA: Why are you trusting us ?

ASHOK: *(To Sneha, jokingly)* Now it is your job to find that out ! *(To Nancy)* I know Doctor Sharma was fighting against social injustice and political injustice. Dowry was one of them. I know a member of Parliament who promised to me he'd fight it in the Parliament if I can give him one ... single ... solid case of dowry burning ...

SNEHA: *(Teasing him)* What about a liquid case ? How solid should be a solid case ?

ASHOK: *(Jokingly)* A case with proof. Not like yours, where there's no proof no witness...

NANCY: Who is this MP ?

ASHOK: Shukla-ji, Vidur Shukla ...

SNEHA: Oh !

ASHOK: *(Teasing)* The way you're nodding as if you know all of our five hundred seventy MPs !

SNEHA: *(Jokingly)* But, we found out their price, the going rate at which you can buy and sell the MPs in today's market ...

NANCY: I have to bring just 25 million dollars, the price of one building in New York, to buy all the MPs who run democracy in India ...

ASHOK: Not all. You should come and see Mr. Shukla. No one can buy him. There are a few more like him in the Parliament ...

Ashok took the risk of escorting them to the Parliament House next day. They were walking in a wide hallway with the individual offices of the Members of Parliament on either side. One door was marked "YASH-PAL KAPOOR, MEMBER OF PARLIAMENT". Yashpal was coming from the other side when he crossed the team of Ashok, Sneha and Nancy. Yashpal stopped and watched where the Police Officer was leading a white girl and found that they had stopped in front of a door marked "VIDUR SHUKLA, MEMBER OF PARLIAMENT". Ashok knocked at the door.

Nancy was very much impressed by the old man, Shukla.

SHUKLA: *(Joking)* 25 million dollars ? That's all ? I didn't know that was the going price of India's democracy in today's market !

NANCY: *(Apologetically)* I'm sorry, sir, I was only joking !

SHUKLA: No, no, no, you don't have to apologize ! That's a fact ! Only we don't have the courage to admit it, or to face it. The country was not like this all the time.

NANCY: That's what I was wondering.

SHUKLA: I was a young volunteer with Mahatma Gandhi. Ashok's father was a senior volunteer, he was older than me. He died almost in poverty. I don't have money to run my campaign. Money is so powerful in India today ! In the days of Mahatma Gandhi, the moral strength was most powerful, not money.

ASHOK: We can always revive the moral strength, can't we ?

SHUKLA: Yes, we can. If we could fight against the British with moral force, we can definitely fight against today's degeneration. But not without sacrifice. *(To Ashok)* What you're doing today is unique. I've not heard a single case where an IAS or IPS officer is ready to sacrifice his career to fight injustice.

SNEHA: Do you think Ashok will be in some trouble ?

SHUKLA: Most likely. You have to be careful, Ashok !

ASHOK: I understand that. However, I'm getting transferred to a local outpost in New Delhi. I'll have more contact with public there.

SHUKLA: For the sake of your career, you must be more careful over there.

ASHOK: I'll bring one dowry burning case with proof to you, as I promised earlier. We will talk about being careful after that.

That evening, while Sneha and Nancy were having their daily girl-talk, Sneha could not resist asking a question she had been holding for more than twenty-four hours.

SNEHA: I was really surprised at you yesterday.

NANCY: Why ?

SNEHA: You watched Neel's wedding and you weren't not upset at all !

NANCY: What's there to be upset with Neel ? He is a scamp. A dwarf that's too big to be a mouse and too small to be a human being. I should have known that earlier. *(A pause)* Forget about him. Let's go to Kathmandu. I'll take care of him later.

SNEHA: *(Fearfully)* Wha … what do you mean by that ?

Nancy took out the perfume dispenser from her bag.

NANCY: I'll shoot him with this !

SNEHA: Oh my God, where did you find that pistol ?

NANCY: *(Laughed)* This is not a pistol ! See ...*(She pulled the trigger. A mist of perfume was dispensed.)* Perfume !

SNEHA: *(Much relieved, she laughed)* Oh, you really scared me ! That looks like a real gun !

NANCY: How cold is Kathmandu ? Will you need winter clothing ?

SNEHA: Do you want me to go with you ?

NANCY: Yes, of course ! You're the one who worked for Doctor Sharma !

SNEHA: *(Hesitating)* Well, I don't know whether I could go ... I've got a problem ...

NANCY: *(Looked at Sneha)* If you don't have money for the air ticket, you don't have to worry. I'll pay for everything. You're helping me in my thesis. I'm going to get all expenses for my thesis work later. *(A pause)* Is there any other problem ?

SNEHA: *(Smiled)* No !

NANCY: All right. Let us get ready. I'll go to my hostel to pick up my stuff, make a few telephone calls, and then I'll be back ...

When Nancy arrived the "INTERNATIONAL STUDENTS' HOSTEL, DELHI UNIVERSITY", a surprise was waiting for her at the lobby. It was Nick, one of the bodyguards of Mr. Agnitti.

NANCY: *(Very surprised)* Nick ? What on earth are you doing here ?

With a broken voice and with the outlook of a human being who was at the edge of his suffering, Nick said, "Boss sent me over here. I have been waiting in this lobby every day for last four days. Nobody can tell me where have you been !"

NANCY: Where are you staying ?

NICK: In another hotel. Can I talk to you in private ?

NANCY: Come to my room.

In Nancy's room, Nick sat down on a chair, far away from Nancy's bed, where she was seated.

NICK: Boss wants you to come back home.

NANCY: I told him over the phone ! I've a lot of data to collect for my thesis.

NICK: How long will it take ?

NANCY: I don't know ! Two months, I guess !

NICK: He didn't find you on the telephone, so he got worried ...

NANCY: I've got to go from place to place to collect the data for my thesis. Tell him not to worry ...

NICK: I don't tell him nothing. He tells me. You should talk to him directly by telephone, if you don't want me to lose my job !

NANCY: You can't call from any place other than New Delhi ! This not like the USA !

NICK: All right, here's something for you ... *(took out a bundle of dollar bills)* Ten grand. Call him up and tell him you got it.

NANCY: Ten grand ! What for ?

NICK: For your expenses.

NANCY: How did you bring the money ? The customs won't allow ...

Nick took out a full size revolver with silencer and showed it to Nancy.

NICK: These Customs guys won't allow this in either !

NANCY: I don't need it ! I have my own gun ...

She took out her perfume dispenser and showed it to Nick.

NICK: We know about that gun. Boss was very mad at Gaggliano for giving you that pea-shooter that can't stop even a mouse at ten feet. He told me to take that back.

Nick took the perfume dispenser and gave the full-size revolver to Nancy.

NICK: You can target practice right in your room. The silencer is so good even the guy in the next room won't hear it.

Nancy fiddled with the revolver for a while. "And, it will stop a mouse at ten feet ?", she asked.

NICK: It'll stop a pig at thirty-five feet.

After Nick left, Nancy ransacked her box, took out a photograph of Neel and arranged it on the desk. Sitting on her bed, she pointed her new pistol at Neel on the photograph. She did not realize how long she was holding the pistol like that. In her mind's eye, the photograph enlarged into Neel in real life.

At Neel's house, however, Neel and Laxmi were being received as newly married husband and wife. Wedding music. Many guests attended the ceremony. Even Sona, the servant girl, had a new dress. Sona was very busy taking care of the bride. There was an instant friendship between Laxmi and Sona, who smiled and liked each other. Reena viewed this with contempt, keeping her distance all the time.

Makkhanlal could not wait for long at his house. He had to rush to attend a secret meeting of the party heads, for which Tyagi also came from Moradabad.

PHULRAJ: *(To Yashpal)* That's what I was saying. There will not be enough time to contact you. Things will move very fast. The moment the Bhinderwala group is arrested, you'll have to go to the Parliament and make the speech.

YASHPAL: Which one ? Blaming the Sikhs for rioting ?

PHULRAJ: *(Exasperated)* No ! No ! Not that ! The one to say that Indira Gandhi is indispensable .... only Nehru family can give stable leadership ....

YASHPAL: Oh, ... that speech is ready, I'll quote from history, with quotation from Mahatma Gandhi and Nehru ... that the only person who could give a stable government in India was Nehru, ... and today ... this person is ... his worthy daughter ... Indira Gandhi !

Everyone clapped.

TYAGI: That's splendid ! The opposition parties will be crushed by that speech.

MAKKHANLAL: If the opposition newspapers again criticize us, do you think we could charge them with sedition ?

PHULRAJ: Sure we can ! You know that the Asian Olympic Games are being organized in New Delhi. Heads of 26 foreign nations will be here. If anybody criticizes the government at this time, that will be sedition !

YASHPAL: Do you want me to add that in my speech ?

PHULRAJ: Yes, of course ! But, please be careful not to give that out before the actual arrival of the foreign dignitaries.

TYAGI: Well, this may be the good time to hit the Assamese in the East.

MAKKHANLAL: This is the right time ! Hit the Assamese in the East, hit the Sikhs in the West, this is the right time ... the Asiad Olympic Games !

TYAGI: Well, I've a plan for Assam at this time. Check out with Mata-ji and let me know if it is all right.

PHULRAJ: What's that ?

TYAGI: We have supplied automatic weapons to the tribals who are ready to attack the Assamese.

YASHPAL: Did you give them the poison bullets ?

TYAGI: Yes. All the ammunition are poison bullets. But, instead of attacking the Assamese, let them attack the Muslims. If a lot of Muslims are killed, we can pin the blame on the Assamese leaders. These Assamese are very proud that their agitation is non-violent and non-communal. If Muslims are killed, we can give publicity that the agitation was actually nothing but a third class communal violence !

PHULRAJ: That's a good idea. But, how can we do that from New Delhi ... a distance of two thousand miles !

TYAGI: Simple ! All that you have to do from New Delhi will be to ask the Army not to intervene till the party workers give clearance. The rest will be easy. I've got party workers who will incite the tribals to attack the Muslims. Are you going to appoint Farin as the Administrator of Assam ?

PHULRAJ: Farin is already in Assam. He took a big grant to furnish his office in Gauhati. I hope he'll represent Government of India over there with full force. Well, if the party workers can set up something against the Assam Movement, we'll send reporters from the foreign press to cover the story. That will give world-wide publicity to the idea that the Assam Movement was basically a third class religious violence.

MAKKHANLAL: The Foreign Press ? Are you going to relax the special Assam Entry Permit for foreigners ?

YASHPAL: That's a good idea. If Mata-ji agrees, I'll write another speech and show you ahead of time ...

Shekhar and Willy came to receive Nancy and Sneha at the Kathmandu International Airport. Nancy introduced Sneha to Shekhar.

SHEKHAR: Glad to meet you Sneha. This is my friend, Willy.

WILLY: Hi !

SNEHA: Hello ! Have you met Doctor Sharma here in Kathmandu ?

NANCY: Sneha was an assistant of Doctor Sharma. We have his address.

SHEKHAR: *(Surprised)* Where did you get his address ? I couldn't find any info about him over here !

SNEHA: From a very discreet source. Nancy told me that we could confide to you.

SHEKHAR: Thanks, Nancy ! I'm glad your opinion has

improved about us !

Everyone laughed.

NANCY: *(Jokingly)* That's only temporary.

WILLY: *(Jokingly)* To be reviewed every day.

NANCY: Every hour, depends upon how you behave !

SNEHA: Great ! Do you think we could get going ? I'm very anxious about the health of the old man ...

SHEKHAR: Let me have the address ...

Nancy gave him a card with an address.

WILLY: I'll go back to our camp. Jim and Bob will need help.

SHEKHAR: Don't negotiate with the Sherpa leader when I'm not there.

WILLY: OK !

Willy went to his taxi. Shekhar escorted Nancy and Sneha to another taxi.

They paid the taxi off at the bottom of a low hill. Sharma's log cabin was at the top of the hill. He was a sixty-two year old man, with a professional look, busy

216

checking patients who stood in a line. He was being helped by Kancha, a young Nepalese boy. Sharma didn't see Sneha, Nancy and Shekhar as they walked uphill by a walkway around the hill. He saw them only when Kancha drew his attention to the upcoming group.

SHARMA: Sneha ! My daughter !

Sneha came running to him. She kneeled down and touched his feet. Sharma grabbed her, put her back on her feet, touched her forehead, and blessed her.

SNEHA: You are so much thinner ! You must have suffered a lot ! Oh God !

She wiped her eyes.

SHARMA: Wouldn't you introduce me to your friends ?

Inside the log cabin, Nancy and Sneha helped Kancha to make tea for everybody.

SHARMA: I am not surprised. India is a big country, with a magnificent civilization that has survived many onslaughts. The present one is nothing. I am sure people will rise. Persons like Ashok will come up, more of them.

NANCY: *(To Sharma)* You do consider an outspoken IPS Officer is a signal for a change ?

SHEKHAR: I do. I would not have believed this if I didn't hear it from you.

SHARMA: What else did he say ?

SNEHA: The Government of India asked the Nepal Government to extradite you, but Nepal turned it down.

SHARMA: *(Happily)* Did they ? That's good. Now I can go back and check my patients.

SNEHA: What about your newspaper ? You always believed in getting a thousand doctors started instead of you alone !

SHARMA: *(Jokingly)* You can see that I was just waiting for you ! Now that you're here, I'll start the journal right away ! *(To Nancy and Shekhar)* She was my right hand person in that news paper work !

NANCY: But you'll need computers, teleprinters, printing machines, and all the other equipment !

SHARMA: I've already talked to some journalists in this country. And, now, God has sent you guys here !

SHEKHAR: What do you want us to do ?

SHARMA: Everything ! Just find your work. Make a Himalayan list of the work to be done and get started ! *(To Nancy)* That's a way of talking over here ! Whenever we've something big to do, we call it Himalayan ! In fact, there is a book called "The Himalayan Blunder " !

NANCY: It's interesting ! Shekhar now has one more mountain to climb !

Sharma was struck by the analogy and he laughed heartily.

SHARMA: One more mountain ? Ha ha ha, Shekhar, why not you invite your mountaineering friends over here and let them help you climb this mountain ?

SHEKHAR: This mountain is not theirs. This mountain is for you to climb, and for Mr. Shukla in New Delhi.

Mr. Shukla, in New Delhi, was, however, bogged down in a back seat in the Parliament, listening to a fiery, patriotic speech of another Member of the Parliament, Yashpal Kapoor.

YASHPAL: *(In the midst of his speech)* Because of the betrayal of the Opposition Parties, the country has gone to the hell. If we look towards the West, what do we see over there ? The Sikhs have been misled by the Opposition Parties to all kind of mischief. They have forgotten all religious tolerance, and are vilifying Hindu temples with cow-heads. I'm sorry to note that the Opposition Parties are instigating both sides to riot. If we look into the East, we see that the Opposition Parties, in cooperation with the American CIA, are instigating the Assamese barbarians to attack the Indians. The whole country is in turmoil because of these unscrupulous people. During the time of such unprecedented turbulence, only Indira Gandhi can give a stable government to the country. If you look at the history, you'll find that Indira Gandhi comes from a family which has been leading the country continuously in the path of stability and peace ..."

The speech was long. Some members fell asleep right in their seats in the Parliament.

Sharma's log cabin, meanwhile, was alive with activities. Workers were unloading a satellite disc and lifting it to the roof for mounting. A van arrived and the driver unloaded some boxes. Sneha came over. In response to the driver's question, she said, "Are those the Encyclopedias ? Put them on that rack !"

Nancy came running ...

NANCY: Sneha, Sneha, the telephone is working ! The telephone is working ! Come over here ...

To get a telephone working appeared to be a great event in Kathmandu at that time. Nancy dragged Sneha to another room. In this room, there was a telephone on one desk and a computer on another.

NANCY: I'm going to call my uncle. What time it'll be in Boston at this time ?

Nancy dialled a lot of numbers.

SNEHA: *(Shaking her head)* Your uncle cannot get any sleep because of you !

NANCY: Will you go and tell Doctor Sharma about the telephone !

Sneha went out only to find that Sharma was having a lot of fun with Jim, Willy, Bob and Shekhar down at the bottom of the hill.

SHARMA: *(Jokingly)* All right. Now you'll see how I climb this hill.

He started to climb, which was quite an ordeal for a sixty-two-year-old ! They all laughed and followed him. Halfway up the hill, Sharma was out of breath. He sat down.

BOB: *(Jokingly)* You're definitely a great climber, Doctor Sharma !

JIM: If you can do this at the age of sixty-two, that's a great inspiration to us.

SHARMA: *(Still trying to breathe)* Oh, I'll do anything to inspire you guys !

Sneha caught up to them at this point. She was herself somewhat out of breath running downhill so fast.

SNEHA: What has happened to you ?

Sharma pointed to a flask of water. Sneha poured

water in a glass and held it for him.

Back in the cabin, Nancy got her connection to her uncle in the USA.

NANCY: *(To the telephone)* Uncle Vinny ! I'm in Nepal now, that telephone number I gave you has the country code 977, city code 1, *(Pause)* ... I'm all right, Uncle Vinny, perfectly all right, it's beautiful up here. Will you send Nick with twenty grand, *(Pause)* ... Nick is down with diarrhea ? OK, ... send Freddie, ask him to call me from the hotel *(Pause)* ... Yes, twenty grand, not a penny less ... it's expensive out here, Uncle Vinny, you know that ...

Down on the slope, Sharma and his group were climbing again.

SHARMA: I want to go faster to see my new telephone up there !

SNEHA: Go slower, will you, please !

Up in the living room, it was tea time. Sneha and Nancy were serving snacks, aided by Kancha.

SHARMA: This is the typical afternoon tea we learnt from the British !

BOB: How many more things did you learn from those Rummies !

Jim signalled Bob not to use that kind of language. Sharma laughed.

SHARMA: I know ! You Americans, particularly the descendants of the Boston Tea Party, have a tendency to talk like that about British. We Indians are different. Although we fought against British for our independence and there were a few atrocities like Jalinwala-bagh, the two hundred years of British administration were like a breeze compared to the seven hundred years of Islamic rule.

BOB: Seven hundred years under Islam ?

SHARMA: 664 years to be exact. From 1193 to 1857 AD. Islamic rule started in Delhi in 1193. They expanded fast, reaching Bengal by 1200 AD. They destroyed all non-Islamic temples and cultural centers, including the great Nalanda University in Bihar. Those who could fight, died. Those who could not, were brutalized. The non-muslims could not protect their women, not to speak of property and other rights. The only way to survive was to take conversion to Islam, or to help the Islamic invaders. The British did not do any such thing. The British were a civilized people. Even a non-violent agitation survived under British.

SHEKHAR: Well, what about the Aryans ? People who

came from Mount Caucasus some six or seven thousand years ago ? They were outsiders, too !

SHARMA: Yes. But, the great Indian culture assimilated those ancient Aryans, and they became a part of India. On the contrary, for various reasons, Islam did not integrate with India. That's why in 1947, Islam took partition from India, and a part of India became an Islamic country, Pakistan.

BOB: What about those Rum...er... British ?

SHARMA: When the British came to India, Indians had already suffered degradation under Islam for six centuries. It was a comparatively easy task for the British. All that they had to do was to play the political game of "divide and rule" !

JIM: And, British left India in 1947 ?

SHARMA: Yes. India got independence from England in 1947. India never got independence from Islam.

SHEKHAR: *(In a tone of a mild protest)* Well, some of the Islamic rulers were very generous, like Nashiruddin, Akbar, ...

SHARMA: That's correct. Islam and Muslim are not the same word, the spelling is different, the meaning is different. Islam means a dogma, Muslim means a human being. There is something in human nature that cannot stop love and compassion, no matter what is the dogma. When the Hindus degenerated during the 664 years of Islamic rule,

225

many generous Muslims, and a few of them were even the Rulers, tried to protect the Hindus from the downfall. However, their generosity towards non-Muslims was in violation of Islam. Islam does not allow any generosity to non-believers. The problem with the Islamic rule in India was that, if one ruler was humanistic, ten would be fanatic. Akbar was so great that he abolished the Jizyah tax which the non-muslims pay in the Islamic countries even today.

NANCY: That's correct ! I heard that from an Egyptian Christian. Even today, Christians pay Zizyah tax in Egypt.

SHARMA: Akbar died in 1605. Just three years later, in 1608, the next Emperor ordered the killing of the Sikh Guru Arjundev, who was roasted alive, according to the encyclopedia. The son of the next emperor re-imposed the Jizyah tax. In the history of 664 years, Jizyah tax was off only for some 90 years.   At least 85% of the 664 years were the history of tyranny and oppression.

JIM: Well, you're too quick to place blame on Islam.

SHARMA: That's not true. Personally, I have deep respect for Prophet Muhammad. Like Shivaji, the Hindu King who rebelled against the Mughals, I respect Koran. But, I do blame the Islamic invaders. I blame the Islamic Rulers. It is not possible to ignore the facts.

JIM: No matter how good the facts are, it is ungenerous to put the blame on Islam.

SHARMA: You don't want to face the facts ? 600-year-old facts may be open to dispute, but what about modern history ? Islam started the first genocide of this century by killing 2 million Armenian Christians in Turkey in the years 1915 and 1916 !

BOB: 2 million Christians ? In 1915 ? How come we don't know anything about it ?

SHARMA: That was the First Genocide of our century. The Second Genocide of our century was the killing of 6 million Jews by Hitler in the 1940's. That became a world news, because Nazism is politics, it is not a religion. Islam passes as a religion, and people don't want to speak against a religion and appear narrow-minded.

BOB: Do you think Hitler drew his inspiration from the Armenian Genocide ?

SHARMA: Maybe. These are the ongoing tragedies of mankind. Even in this decade, in 1981, ten thousand Chakma Buddhists were massacred by the Islamic Army in Bangladesh. Nobody complained, because it appears ungenerous to speak against Islam.

SHEKHAR: It is difficult to accept that a man of your spiritual attainments would be so quick to place blame on Islam.

SHARMA: I don't have any spiritual attainments ! I'm a very ordinary man. That's why I can't ignore the facts.

SHEKHAR: *(Apologetically)* I'm sorry, I didn't mean to say that. All that I'm concerned is the continuation of the cycle of violence. Revenges. If you blame Islam, Muslims in India will suffer from violence ...

SHARMA: I'm opposed to any kind of violence ... any kind of revenges. If I can find a single Hindu organization that professes violence against Muslims, I'll oppose it. Hindu organizations do not profess violence. In fact, the Indian Muslims were the first victims of Islam in India. Their ancestors were forced to accept Islam at the point of the sword. Today, it is the duty of every Hindu to protect their Muslim brothers from any kind of violence. India got independence from England without hurting a single Anglo-Indian. India can also get independence from Islam without hurting a single Indian Muslim. Hindus must remember that the Indian Muslims were their brothers, lost in the hurricane of history. When the hurricane is over, the two brothers will reunite.

Nancy was silent during the debate. Now she levelled her gaze at Jim and asked, "You started the whole thing. Why do you think nobody should blame Islam ? Is it some kind of a holy cow ?"

Sharma laughed at Nancy's strong stand. "It's not Jim's fault, Nancy ! Everybody takes Islam as just another religion. But, Islam is not just another religion. It is politics. It is a doctrine of fanatic supremacy. For example, when Pakistan was created in 1947, there was an agreement between India and Pakistan that both the countries would protect their minorities."

NANCY: Did they ?

SHARMA: In 1947, at the time of partition, there were

44% non-Muslims in East Pakistan, now called Bangladesh. Today, that number has reduced to less than 10%.

NANCY: What about West Pakistan ?

SHARMA: In 1947, at the time of partition, there were 23% non-Muslims in West Pakistan. Today, there are less than 1% non-Muslim in West Pakistan.

JIM: I didn't know they are all wiped out ! What happened in India ?

SHARMA: There were 11% Muslim in India in 1947. Today, the Muslim population in India has increased to 19%.

SHEKHAR: That's why you said Islam is more politics and less religion ?

SHARMA: Verify the numbers. Correct me if I'm wrong. Dig up the facts. Then, try to look at it on the basis of facts !

Willy, the veritable "manager", tried to change the subject. "Well, Doctor Sharma, you said you'd do anything to inspire us in our effort to climb the Himalayan mountains ..."

SHARMA: *(Jokingly)* I even climbed with you today, didn't I ...

WILLY: I know ! That was very generous. But will you please do us one more favor ?

SHARMA: What's that ?

WILLY: Will you permit us to put your name down as the medical officer of our team ? I mean, you don't have to climb with us, we just have to be able to use your name ...

SHARMA: Why ?

SHEKHAR: I know what Willy is trying to say. We must show the name of a licensed medical practitioner as our medical officer ...

WILLY: But, we don't have the funds to hire one.

SHARMA: *(Enthusiastically)* Oh, in that case, I'll always help. I may not have money to donate, but my services ... I'll even climb with you !

SNEHA: What about your own health ?

SHARMA: *(Lovingly)* Oh Sneha, now that you're here, I know I don't have any independence ...

Laxmi was too young and too inexperienced to understand why everybody was so cool towards her in her husband's house. She did know that her father could not pay her dowry in full, but a payment plan acceptable to both the parties had been agreed to. But that, apparently, did not warm up Laxmi's in-laws, not even her husband.

"When are you going to get the wedding photographs ? All my friends in Miranda College are bugging me ..." , Laxmi tried her best to be intimate with Neel.

"Photographs are expensive, you know ! The color prints !", Neel was very cool.

This was embarrassing for a newly married girl. "Well, if you don't mind, I'll tell my father to give the money ..."

"Your father didn't give even a refrigerator as promised, and now you want photographs ...", Neel gibed.

Laxmi protested. "He gave a refrigerator !"

231

Neel replied in a tone that sounded like an insult, "Yeah. He gave an Indian Elwin refrigerator. Not even a Godrej. He was supposed to give a foreign made Westinghouse, or at least a Kenmore or a Maytag. I'm so ashamed in front of my family members !"

Neel's family members, on the other hand, were having their secret conference in the living room, in hushed voices.

TARA: Even some of the jewelry are fake !

MAKKHANLAL: Who told you that ?

REENA: I took a few pieces to the goldsmith. The man started to laugh at me. I was so ashamed !

Reena stopped when she saw Sona entering with a tray of snacks and tea. No one talked while Sona kept the tray on the center table.

TARA: *(To Sona)* Where's the new bride ?

SONA: I don't know, Memsahib ! May I take her to Kornel Uncle's house, Memsahib ?

TARA: Do the dishes first. Run !

Sona virtually ran out of the room.

REENA: *(To Sona)* Shut the door behind you.

They started to talk after the door was shut.

MAKKHANLAL: *(Sipping tea)* I don't worry about the jewelry very much as long as he comes up with the cash installment in time.

TARA: How much he was supposed to pay this month ?

MAKKHANLAL: Twenty-five thousand.

TARA: That was from last month. So this month it should be fifty thousand.

REENA: Why are you trying to cover up for their family, Papa ?

TARA: How do you plan to pay Reena's in-laws if you keep on covering for Laxmi's father ?

Makkhanlal tried to persuade his wife and daughter to forgive his new daughter-in-law, but he did not succeed. The anxiety over making the payment to Reena's in-laws was looming heavily in their minds. Tara and Reena did not touch their tea.

TARA: What answer do you have ? How do you plan to send Reena back to her in-laws if you don't get all the money you owe them next month ?

MAKKHANLAL: *(Defensively)* I'm getting more time.

Phulraj promised me, he'd talk to them, and get me more time ...

TARA: Phulraj also promised to send that ugly, retired Colonel to jail ! He didn't keep that promise, either !

REENA: *(To Makkhanlal)* Why don't you ask Mr. Dwivedi to come up with the money ? That was the deal with him, wasn't it ?

When Makkhanlal arrived at the office of Phulraj Mathur, Phulraj was on the telephone. Some assistants were busying themselves with office functions --- bringing in papers to sign, filing, taking signed documents away, etc.

PHULRAJ: *(To the telephone)* Yes, I got the telegram. Did he send you a copy ?

The other end of the telephone was at the Army Headquarters. General Vohra, a senior Army General who was the GOC, General Officer in Command, Eastern Sub-area Commands, was trying to cut corners with the Prime Minister's Office over the telephone.

234

GOC: *(To the telephone)* No. I didn't get any telegram from any civilian officer. My info came from the Army's Situation Report this morning ... how can I sit tight when the situation is so tense ...

PHULRAJ: *(To the telephone)* You don't worry about it. These are political matters. Army must not move until we give clearance.

GOC: *(To the telephone)* To hell with all these politics ! Twenty thousand tribals have mobilized in the hills with bows and arrows and hatchets, their drums are beating day and night, and you don't want me to move the Army to the position ? What'll happen if they come down to the plains and start attacking people ? *(A long pause)* All right, you give me that in writing. I don't want to be blamed later on.

Phulraj put his telephone down. An Assistant was taking notes from Phulraj.

PHULRAJ: *(To the Assistant #1)* Issue the entry permits for foreign reporters to enter Assam. Make sure they take TV cameras. Make sure foreign exchange is available to buy films and videotapes.

The Assistant of Phulraj Mathur was trying his best to contain his excitement.

ASSISTANT #1: Do you think the massacre will occur as planned ?

PHULRAJ: I'm sure. *(To Assistant #2)* Is the statement

ready ?

Assistant #1 went out.

ASSISTANT #2: It's almost ready. I sent one copy to Yashpal-ji. He'll be here any minute.

PHULRAJ: All right. Now you work on the Sikh problem. Complete that statement about Bhinderwala.

ASSISTANT #2: Yes sir.

Assistant #2 went out. Phulraj now got some time to talk to Makkhanlal.

PHULRAJ: Yes, Makkhanlal !

MAKKHANLAL: I came for a personal problem ...

Yashpal entered at this time. Makkhanlal became silent.

YASHPAL: *(Excitedly)* What's the news ?

PHULRAJ: *(Smiling)* Perfect as planned ! Our agents must be appreciated ! They worked day and night in those Assam hills and mobilized the tribals. The tribals are now coming down.

YASHPAL: When are you sending the foreign reporters to Assam ?

PHULRAJ: In right time ! When the news hits the world

press, that'll be the end of the Assam Movement. Do you have her statement ready ?

YASHPAL: Yes. Over here. In this statement, all the violence will be pinned on the leaders of the so called "non-violent" Assam Movement.

Yashpal passed a paper to Phulraj.

PHULRAJ: That's great. Now you have to help me on that Sikh problem ...

A special telephone, marked "P.M.", started to ring. Phulraj picked it up with great respect.

PHULRAJ: *(To the telephone)* Yes, Mata-ji !

Phulraj stood up as a token of respect.   Yashpal and Makkhanlal also stood up in reflex action.

PHULRAJ: *(To the telephone)* Yes, Mata-ji, I'm coming Mata-ji ! *(To Yashpal)* Please wait ! She may call you ! *(To Makkhanlal)* I'll talk about your personal problem later on. Please come at some other time.

Phulraj left the room in a haste.

In the mean time, Sharma's office in Kathmandu had been endowed with a few extra telephones and computers. A teleprinter was printing the wire-service messages in another room, giving the atmosphere of a newspaper office. Sneha, Nancy and a few other workers were busy helping Sharma. Shekhar, Willy, Jim and Bob were not there. They had gone to practice in the Himalayas.

SHARMA: *(Reading a teleprinter)* I don't believe this ! Indira Gandhi is openly inciting Bhinderwala against the Akaali Sikhs !

NANCY: What's an Akaali ?

SHARMA: Oh ! That's an ancient word, meaning "timelessness". "Kaala" means "Time", "Akaala" means "Timeless". It is the reminder of an ancient philosophy which saw an "Absolute State of Existence" beyond the cause and effect of Time and Space ...

NANCY: And ... did you say that's the name of a

political party ?

SHARMA: Everything is political in India today ! That's why I'm going to name my journal "India Tomorrow" ! We have to go back to the future !

SNEHA: Bapuji *(meaning Sharma)*, do you want to print Saxena's report in this issue ?

SHARMA: Oh yes ! And thanks, Nancy, for bringing that report to me.

NANCY: Do you think it will put Colonel Saxena in some jeopardy ?

SHARMA: Don't worry about the Colonel. He is a strong military man. He is from the artillery. His nickname was Karak Bijli.

NANCY: What's that ?

SHARMA: "The Blasting Thunder". That was the name of a cannon the Queen of Jhansi used against the British.

NANCY: And now ?

SHARMA: Now, the enemy is within.

SNEHA: I got a telephone call from Ashok.

NANCY: Oh, yes ? What did he say ?

SNEHA: He has mobilized all the reporters and distributors for our newspaper. He also organized the truck services to distribute the newspaper from Biratnagar to all the distribution centers in India.

SHARMA: That's just a dream come true. We will be very busy now !

NANCY: *(To Sharma)* Will you have time to answer my questions ? I ... I have so many of them !

SHARMA: *(Jokingly)* I've seen your list of questions ! What is your question today ?

NANCY: Doctor Sharma, I've nothing to hide from you. I was about to be married to a Hindu boy. They rejected me because they were strict vegetarian. According to them, every living being is an image of God. To kill a living being for food ...

SHARMA: Wait a minute, Nancy ! *(To Sneha)* Sneha, will you please bring the Encyclopedia, number 9.

NANCY: *(To Sharma)* The Hindus don't kill an animal for food, but they burn innocent brides for dowry. Will you please tell me, what does the Hinduism stand for ?

SHARMA: That's a wonderful combination: vegetarianism on one hand, burning of a girl on the other ! Let us try to collect some data. Do you know that burning of girls for dowry is prevalent only in the Indo-Gangetic Plains. There is no dowry burning in the hills of Nepal, Assam or in the hills of South India.

241

NANCY: *(Surprised)* No ?

SHARMA: *(Pointing to a map in encyclopedia)* Come here. Look at this map ...

When Nancy came closer, Sharma pointed to a map of India in 1605.

SHARMA: This is the map of Islamic India of 1605. Nepal and Assam were outside this map. South India was very loosely ruled. The stronghold of the Islamic rulers was the Indo-Gangetic plains.

Nancy pointed to the map in the Encyclopedia. "This shaded part was the Islamic India ?"

SHARMA: That's the Indo-Gangetic Plains. The strength of Islam was in cavalry. The vast plains were at their mercy. But, they did not succeed in the mountainous regions of Assam, Nepal or Maharastra. Dowry burning is a custom only in these parts of India which were ruled by Islamic invaders for 664 years. Assam and Nepal were never ruled by Islam. There is no dowry burning in Assam or Nepal, even today.

NANCY: That's very interesting ! How do you connect Dowry with the Islamic Rule ? In Islam, the women are suppressed, but Muslims don't have any bride burning !

SHARMA: Hindus were second class people under Islamic rule, not the Muslims ! Hindus degenerated under Islamic rule, not the Muslims. Try to imagine the scenario in history. The Islamic invaders occupied Delhi in 1193

242

AD and sent the cavalry to the countryside to crush the non-Islamic people. Those who fought, died. Others ran away. Those who survived and surrendered and wanted to survive in the Islamic India had to plead that they were meek and mild and harmless vegetarian people who might be allowed to cling to life at no danger to the Rulers.

NANCY: That's how vegetarianism became a vogue ? As a shield of protection ??

SHARMA: Hinduism is not vegetarianism. In true Hinduism, everything depends upon what is your duty at that post of life. The Kshatriyas, the fighting class, were given to hunting and non-vegetarianism even in the time of Mahabharata and Geeta. In fact, there was a book called "Vyaadha Geeta", meaning the "Geeta of the Hunters". Vegetarianism is not prevalent among Hindus in non-Islamic India. Gurkhas of Nepal and the fighters in the hills of Maharastra and Assam are not vegetarian. These areas were outside Islamic rule.

NANCY: That's very interesting !

SHARMA: Those who wanted to survive under the Islamic rule had no choice but to plead that they were absolutely docile, vegetarian people, ready to pay any tax for their survival, that they would not fight and would not cause any trouble.

NANCY: That sounds like the pre-Christian Britons under Roman rule.

SHARMA: Worse than that ! These non-Islamic Indians who were clinging to life as second class people under the

Islamic rule, couldn't protect their daughters. During the 664 years of Islamic Rule, the soldiers could enter any house of a non-Islamic family and snatch away the grown up daughter and take her to the harem of the Sultan. To save their honor, hordes of women used to jump into burning pyres. This was called a Vrata, a vow, called "Jahar Vrata", or the "Vow of Poison", "Vow of Purity" or the "Vow of Death".

NANCY: Oh my God !

SHARMA: This went on for hundreds of years. Millions of women died in the "Jahar Vrata". During those 664 years, burning of a Hindu woman became an acceptable scenario in Islamic India. Since that scenario ran for hundreds of years, it became a second nature of the Hindus in Islamic India. Even today, Hindus in the Indo-Gangetic Plains do not feel strongly that it is a crime to burn a woman. In early British Rule, this transformed into Suttee Burning. There was no Suttee Burning or bride burning or woman burning among the Hindus in the non-Islamic parts of India.

SNEHA: I never thought of it in that light !

SHARMA: For 664 years, the Hindus in Islamic India could not protect their daughters. To save family prestige, the only way out was to pass the buck to another family. That's how child marriage started. The father of a female child would go to the father of a male child and beg him to marry his daughter to his son. The father of the boy, who had received several offers for his son, would accept the highest bidder. When such a condition continued for 664 years, no wonder they forgot how the dowry system

244

started in the first place.

NANCY: My God ! That explains it ! Child marriage was a part of the dowry system !

SHARMA: Child marriage was also responsible for a thwarted growth of the individual and the exclusiveness of the caste system, and many other social evils. People who refused to live a life of a second class citizen in Islamic India ran away and took shelter in Nepal and Assam. Nepal is not a part of political India today. During those 664 years of debasement, Assam was the only India left outside of Islamic overlordship. In that encyclopedia, you see the phrase "Except Assam" many times in the history of Islamic India. Assam was actually "India-in-exile" for 664 years.

SNEHA: Mahatma Gandhi wrote an article "Lovely Assam" many years ago !

SHARMA: Today the politicians are burning Assam in another dowry burning.

NANCY: I was all the time wondering, if the Hindus are so spiritual that they won't even kill a chicken for food, how could they burn a girl for dowry ?

SHARMA: It's not spirituality. Didn't you see the display of currency notes in the wedding rituals ?

NANCY: Yes ! That was my next question. In the wedding rituals that I saw, I found that the Brahmin priest started the discussions on dowry deals, as if that was a part of the scriptures. Are those things written in the

Hindu scriptures ?

SHARMA: No. There is no mention of dowry in Hindu scriptures. These Brahmin priests are the greatest criminals. It is their duty to declare a marriage null and void if it is polluted by a dowry deal.

NANCY: Instead of that, they initiate the discussion of money ! How does money become such an important part of a wedding ritual ?

SHARMA: Well, you have to remember the same scenario. In spite of the power of Islamic cavalry and sword, in spite of the "mercenary" Hindu soldiers who worked for the Islamic Masters for a salary, the vast majority of the Hindu population managed to stay away from a formal conversion to Islam by accepting a second class status, by degrading themselves, by paying a special tax, called Jizyah Tax, that the non-Muslims pay in Islamic countries even today. But, to collect the taxes and to rule over them, the Islamic rulers needed defectors, turncoats and time-servers. These time-servers would work in the Islamic Courts, collect money from the non-Muslim subjects and take the same to their Islamic masters. "Nehru" was the official designation of the tax collector of a "Nehar", that means a canal. These money collectors paid only a part of the money to their Islamic masters and kept a good part for themselves. They amassed vast sums of money over the hundreds of years --- maybe three hundred years --- and passed it on to their descendants. To gain the confidence of their Islamic masters, these time-servers would get some of their relatives converted to Islam. These money collectors were the most powerful men in the society during the 664 years, supported openly by the Islamic rulers. But there were another kind of money "collectors" who were supported indirectly by the Islamic rulers. One such sect was called the "Thug", or the "Deceivers".

NANCY: I heard about a movie by that name !

SNEHA: *(Critically)* Do you mean to say that the Islamic rulers supported the Thugs ?

SHARMA: Not directly. But, there must have been an indirect support. Otherwise ... explain to me ... how could the Thugs operate in full force for about three hundred years under Islamic rule ?

NANCY: Are they still there ?

SHARMA: No. British eradicated the Thugs in just six years between 1831-1837. Before that, the Thugs were operating for 300 years in Islamic India, in the Indo-gangetic plains. There was no sect of Thugs in Assam or in Nepal, or in non-Islamic India.

SNEHA: I never thought in that line !

SHARMA: Being devoid of other values of life like independence and self respect, money became the symbol of power and pride in Islamic India. Any kind of currency became the most beautiful object of life.

NANCY: I saw one bridegroom wearing a garland made of big rupee notes !

SHARMA: Were you surprised ?

SNEHA: I wasn't ! I've seen it from my childhood. I never thought there was anything wrong in it !

NANCY: Like Doctor Asthana who never thought there was anything wrong in burning the girls for dowry.

SHARMA: Now you know the roots of dowry burning. Nancy, you've got to realize one thing: when something goes on for 664 years, people forget how it got started. It becomes a part of life. It becomes a deep-rooted disease ...

NANCY: How do you cure it ?

SHARMA: I am a doctor. I have just diagnosed the disease. I have not figured out the cure, not yet !

SNEHA: You must have some idea !

SHARMA: It is like curing a sick lion who doesn't remember its own strength. Indian Civilization reached its pinnacle some five thousands years ago. It saw the light ... the truth of Adwaita that gave the great teaching of "Vasudhaiva Kutumbakam" ....

NANCY: *(Interrupting)* What's its meaning ?

SHARMA: It means, "The entire world is your kith and kin" ...

NANCY: Ah ! That's beautiful ! But ...

SHARMA: But, what ?

NANCY: *(Skeptically)* If the entire world is kith and kin, what about the caste system among the Hindus that excludes one caste from another ?

SHARMA: Originally ... I mean some three thousand years before Christ ... caste system was a division of labor. It was occupational, not hereditary. A man or a woman was free to select a vocation that was suitable to his or her nature and taste and aptitude. It was praised even as late as the Geeta ... which might have been compiled some six hundred years before Christ ... as "Swabhava Dharma" meaning "Duty as per your own nature". However, between 1193 and 1857 ... the 664 years of Islamic domination ... when a child was married at the age of ten, and was asked to carry on the family line, the independence to choose one's own career vanished. Caste system distorted into a hereditary narrowness.

NANCY: How do you cure it ?

SHARMA: By finding out the truth. Truth about ourselves. I want to take my countrymen back to that peak ... the wisdom of Adwaita ... the wisdom of universal love ... without any distinction between caste and creed and national origin ... the wisdom that will remove the darkness of 664 years of debasement.

Back in New Delhi, Ashok decided to caution Colonel Saxena that his report was about to be printed in Sharma's newspaper. Ashok was now the Police Officer in charge of Saxena's neighborhood. He paid a visit to Saxena. The latter opened the door.

ASHOK: Are you Colonel Saxena ?

Ashok was in full Police uniform. Saxena didn't understand why an unknown Police Officer should come to visit him.

SAXENA: Yes ! Any problem ?

ASHOK: No. May I come in, please ?

At the living room, Saxena was watching Ashok critically.

ASHOK: I am posted in the police station of your area. I've some information for you. I hope you don't mind !

SAXENA: What is it ?

ASHOK: Do you remember Doctor Sharma ?

SAXENA: Yes ! Have you guys arrested him ?

ASHOK: No. He is in Kathmandu. He is starting his journal from there. He is going to publish your report in the first issue. If that happens, they may ask me to come here and arrest you.

Saxena was still very suspicious about Ashok. "All right. If that happens, you come here and arrest me. Why are you telling me in advance ?"

ASHOK: Because I don't want to arrest you. I want you to go free and uphold the honor of Mother India.

Saxena looked at Ashok in great surprise. An IPS Officer was not supposed to talk like that !

ASHOK: Do you think I could be of any help ?

SAXENA: I'm surprised. Aren't you an IPS Officer ?

ASHOK: Yes, I am. But, I don't think my IPS position will survive for long. Before they get me, I want to do certain things. Do you think I could be of any help ?

True to his military instinct, Saxena sized up the situation and made his own decision.

"Yes", he told Ashok, "You can help me a lot. When you come to arrest me, give me some time so that I may dress up in my old Army Uniform. I want to walk into the prison in my full Uniform of the Artillery Battalion."

Their conversation, however, was disturbed by Sona and Laxmi who entered from the interiors.

SONA: Uncle, uncle, please see who is here with me ! Remember I told you about Laxmi ? I have brought her to introduce to Aunti-ji !

SAXENA: Oh, so you are Laxmi ! Sona has been talking about you all the time ! She told us you sing very well !

SONA: She used to, at the beginning.

SAXENA: May be we can hear some songs !

SONA: Not any more, Uncle-ji ! For the last month, she has not even hummed once.

LAXMI: Keep quiet, Sona !

SONA: Where is Aunti-ji ? Maybe she will be able to make her sing again !

SAXENA: Your Aunti will be back from the temple very soon.

SONA: Let us go to the kitchen and make tea for the guests, is that all right, Uncle-ji ?

SAXENA: That kitchen is yours, Sona !

Sona and Laxmi went to the kitchen. Saxena told Laxmi, "Laxmi, will you please wait for your Aunti, if you can !"

After they were gone, Ashok asked, "Who is that girl ?"

SAXENA: The talkative one is a student of my wife. She is the servant in our next door neighbor. The quiet one is their new daughter-in-law.

ASHOK: New daughter-in-law ? She is awfully quiet ! Even frightened. What's the matter with her ? Do you have any idea ?

Saxena shrugged. "Don't ask me. I am an outcast here. We were not even invited to the wedding !"

At their base camp in the Himalayas, the mountaineering team was busy working on their schedules. Jim and Bob were practicing on a cliff. Shekhar and Willy were busy organizing the Sherpas.

WILLY: I'm amazed how smoothly you managed those Sherpa leaders !

SHEKHAR: That's very simple. The Sherpas are straightforward, mountain people. I'm glad you have a good rapport with them now.

WILLY: I hope it will last !

SHEKHAR: I'm sure it will. So, if you agree, I'll like to go back to Kathmandu for a few days ...

WILLY: To take care of Nancy ?

SHEKHAR: Come'n Willy, will you stop teasing me ! I'm really worried about Nancy. She has an explosive personality. I don't know what she will do next.

WILLY: Why is that your concern ? Are you in love with her ?

SHEKHAR: No. *(A pause)* I mean, I never thought in that way. I was worried because the way Neel treated her ...

Willy thought Shekhar was trying to avoid the question. He asked him again, "Are you in love with Nancy ?"

Shekhar looked at Willy for some time. Then he replied slowly, "Maybe. I don't know. I'm not sure. But, I am sure of one thing ----- I cannot forget my wife Kamla. The other day ... in that garden ... when I saw those humming birds ... "

"Humming birds ?"

"Those little birds that flip their wings, balance like a tiny helicopter at one spot, and drink the nectar of the flowers with their long beaks ! In our honeymoon, we went to a garden, ... and Kamla was so happy ... running around between the flowers. When she saw a humming bird drinking nectar from a flower, she laughed and laughed and told me --- she would like to turn into a humming bird and drink the nectar of the flowers .... "

Willy paused for a while before changing the subject, "When do you plan to come back ?"

SHEKHAR: Very soon. As soon as possible. I'll join you at your next base camp.

WILLY: Are you going to Moradabad ? To see your father ?

SHEKHAR: No.

Shekhar's father, Tyagi, meanwhile, was busy at the office of Phulraj Mathur in New Delhi. Phulraj was reading the first issue of Sharma's journal, "India Tomorrow". Tyagi and Yashpal were seated across the desk.

PHULRAJ: I don't know how I'll show this to Mata-ji.

YASHPAL: Where's she ?

PHULRAJ: She has gone to receive the Great Emperor Haile Selassie at the airport.

TYAGI: The Heads of twenty-six countries ... Emperors, Presidents, Princes ... great, great people ... are coming to Delhi for the Asiad games, and these traitors are writing these kind of articles at this time ...

Makkhanlal entered at this time.

MAKKHANLAL: *(With a worried look)* May I talk to you for a minute in private, Phulraj-ji ?

PHULRAJ: I don't have time for your private problems at this time, Makkhanlal ! See *(showing the journal)* what your friend Doctor Sharma is writing here ...

MAKKHANLAL: He's not my friend !

Makkhanlal took the paper and read.

YASHPAL: *(To Phulraj)* I thought you asked the Nepal Government to stop him at Kathmandu ...

PHULRAJ: We did. But, the Nepal Government doesn't listen to us.

TYAGI: We must finish this Doctor Sharma, somehow.

MAKKHANLAL: Your own son, Shekhar, is working for Doctor Sharma !

TYAGI: No, he's not ! Don't give out rumors without any proof.

MAKKHANLAL: Shekhar is in Kathmandu, I'm told, isn't he ?

YASHPAL: *(To Makkhanlal)* What about your son ? I'm told he was about to marry the American girl I saw in our enemy's camp the other day !

PHULRAJ: Enemy ? What do you mean ?

YASHPAL: That member of Parliament, Shukla.

PHULRAJ: Forget about Shukla. He is an old man. He will be out of picture very soon. I'm worried about Colonel Saxena. Now that his report is published in Sharma's paper, the good old Colonel may turn into a national hero overnight.

MAKKHANLAL: You must get hold of the Army top brass and finish this retired Colonel as soon as possible.

The telephone rang.

PHULRAJ: *(To the telephone)* Yes ! *(Pause)* General Gulati ? Put him on. *(Pause)* Yes, General, the Prime Minister is not available now. You should talk to the Defence Minister.

The telephone call was from General Gulati of Army Headquarters.

GULATI: *(To the telephone)* The Defence Minister isn't available either. He's gone to inaugurate the Cricket Match with West Indies.

PHULRAJ: *(To the telephone)* What did you want to talk about ?

GULATI: *(To the Telephone)* Did you see Colonel Saxena's report in "India Tomorrow" ?

PHULRAJ: *(To the telephone)* Colonel Saxena is an army men, it is your job to control him !

GULATI: *(To the telephone)* Yes, but you promised you'd suppress that journal. Had I known that you wouldn't, I'd have never suppressed Colonel Saxena's Report. After all, he was one of our finest officers, high character, great courage, high morality, ... every ideal the Army stands for ...

PHULRAJ: *(To the telephone)* I know. Your young Army Officers respect Colonel Saxena, the good old "Karak Bijli" of the Artillery. But, wait and see, what we do to him. And if you keep quiet, I'll make you the Ambassador to Cambodia when you retire next month ... *(Pause)* All right, I'll ring you when Prime Minister returns.

Phulraj hung up.

TYAGI: Did you get the information that the tribals are coming down in Assam ?

PHULRAJ: It's difficult to run something from here at a distance of two thousand miles.

YASHPAL: Are you sure you'll be able to put the blame on the leaders of the non-violent movement of Assam ?

PHULRAJ: The statement is all ready to go. The moment the foreign reporters publish the report, Mata-ji will go to the Parliament and make a statement so that the student leaders of Assam will be held responsible for the violence.

Phulraj picked up the telephone and asked one of

his assistants to come to his office.

"Did the order to issue Assam Entry Permit to Foreign Reporters go out ?", Phulraj asked him.

"Yes sir."

"What about the release of foreign exchange from the Reserve Bank for photographic films and video cassettes ?"

"All done, sir."

"What about that statement to the Parliament ?"

"I gave you that yesterday, sir !"

Phulraj found it in his drawer. "All right, you may go now. Oh, send in the file on Sikh problem."

Phulraj pushed a paper from his drawer to Yashpal.

PHULRAJ: *(To Yashpal)* Here's the copy of the statement you'll have to make in Parliament ...

YASHPAL: Has she seen it ?

PHULRAJ: Do we have time to show all the material ... everything ... to her !

MAKKHANLAL: May I please talk to you, Phulraj-ji ?

PHULRAJ: We are all friends here, aren't we, Makkh-anlal ! Whatever we say here doesn't go out from these four walls. You don't have to talk to me in private.

MAKKHANLAL: But, this is a private family matter.

PHULRAJ: What ? Neel's father-in-law failed to pay the dowry installment ?

MAKKHANLAL: For two months. Now, Reena's father-in-law has refused to give any more time ! Can you talk to him ?

PHULRAJ: Me ? Do you think I have any time for these kind of family matters ?

YASHPAL: Reena's father-in-law is Mr. Wadhwani, isn't he ?

TYAGI: You should not have made any of your relations with a member of opposition party.

PHULRAJ: Why don't you put pressure on Neel's father-in-law ?

Makkhanlal was embarrassed.

MAKKHANLAL: He now frankly says he does not have any money.

PHULRAJ: He should have not made an agreement, in that case !

At this time, Manmohan, another Assistant of

Phulraj, entered with a file.

PHULRAJ: *(To Manmohan)* You're supposed to knock before entering, Manmohan ! What kind of training did you get in your IAS training camp ?

MANMOHAN: I'm sorry, sir ! Here's the Sikh file that you wanted, sir ! I'm afraid I have some bad news for you, sir ! This one just came over the teleprinter, sir !

       Manmohan gave the file and a teleprinter message. Phulraj eyed the message and became alarmed.

PHULRAJ: You may go, Manmohan. *(Passed over the teleprinter message to Yashpal.)*

TYAGI: What's that ?

PHULRAJ: Bhinderwala has taken shelter in the Golden Temple.

YASHPAL: That's no problem ! Send the Army to bombard the Golden Temple.

MAKKHANLAL: Golden Temple ? You want to bomb the Golden Temple of Amritsar ?

TYAGI: What's so great about Golden Temple ? They don't have any right to use it for political purposes !

MAKKHANLAL: We didn't have any right to give machine guns to Bhinderwala and to incite him against the Akali Party !

PHULRAJ: Which side are you belong to, Makkhanlal ? You're talking like an opposition leader.

YASHPAL: How well armed is Bhinderwala, anyway ?

PHULRAJ: I don't know. We gave him enough arms and ammunition to blow up entire Punjab.

TYAGI: Well, if he does any such thing, we'll be able to put the blame on Pakistan, saying that Pakistan gave all these arms and ammunition to Bhinderwala.

MAKKHANLAL: Like you supplied poison bullets to the Bodo tribals in Assam.

TYAGI: Assam Tribals don't need bullets, Makkhanlal ! When they come down in twenty thousands, they smash everything with clubs and hatchets.

When Sharma got the news that foreign Press Reporters were given permission to go to Assam, he became very suspicious.

SHARMA: That's strange ! Are they giving entry permits to the foreign press to go to Assam ?

SNEHA: That's what Ashok said over the telephone.

SHARMA: Did he say anything particularly about the tribal population there ?

SNEHA: No. But, he said he'd call again.

NANCY: What's so special about the tribal population ?

SHARMA: Indira Gandhi's party workers have been spending millions of rupees for a long time to incite the tribals against the Assam Movement. This is the first time they're allowing foreign press to go into Assam. I think she's brewing some news there.

SHEKHAR: *(To Nancy)* If you wanted to go to Assam, this is the golden opportunity.

NANCY: I must go there. Shekhar, can you please help me get my plane tickets and visa and ...

SHEKHAR: I'll help you if you allow me to go with you. You can't travel there alone.

SHARMA: I agree with Shekhar. In fact, both of you must be very careful.

SHEKHAR: Well, I know Mr. Farin, the Chief Administrator who rules Assam on behalf of Government of India.

SHARMA: Are you sure he will look after your safety ?

SHEKHAR: He is a close associate of my father. I hope he doesn't know that I've problem with my father !

SHARMA: Well, that's a calculated risk. You ask Mr. Farin to give the police protection on all your travels in Assam. If he doesn't agree to that, come back, don't stay there any longer, either of you.

NANCY: Before I go, I must learn everything about the tribal people.

SHARMA: Well, the tribals are the original inhabitants of India.

SHEKHAR: Like the Red Indians in America.

NANCY: That's interesting !

SHARMA: So are the Dravidians, the dark skinned people of South India. The Aryans entered India through the passes of Hindukush Mountains some five thousand years ago.

NANCY: Five thousand ?

SHARMA: Opinions vary. Maybe ten thousand. Maybe four thousand. Some people believe Aryans didn't come from outside at all. They originated right here in India.

NANCY: Which is the correct theory ?

SHARMA: I don't know ! For the purpose of discussion, let's assume that the Aryans came from Mount Caucasus some six thousand years ago. The Aryans were white, aggressive people. They spread over the Indo-gangetic plains, driving the aboriginal inhabitants to the mountains or to the South. The Gods of the Aryan people, like their language, were very similar to the Roman and Greek Gods. Their language, Sanskrit, is very similar to Latin. On the other hand, the non-Aryans were dark skinned people. Their origin is buried in the remote past. They had a dream theory very similar to the dream theory of the aboriginal Australians. Many of their sects had a Mother God. Many of their sects were matriarchal. Women had extremely high position in their society. Intellectually, they were highly developed.

SHEKHAR: Are you sure there was no Mother God in Aryan Veda ?

SHARMA: The Aryan thoughts were recorded in the three books, called Veda: Rikveda, Yajurveda and Saamaveda. All the three Vedas were not compiled at the same time. The original Veda is the Rik Veda. The other two can be seen as derivatives of Rik Veda. Now, Rik Veda has one major stanza on Mother God, the Devi Sukta. Do you know who the first God is in the first verse of Rik Veda ?

SNEHA: No !

SHARMA: Agni.

NANCY: Agni ? That sounds familiar ! What's the meaning of the word Agni ?

SHARMA: In Sanskrit, it means Fire. The God of Fire. See the similarity with the Latin word "Ignes" which means fire.

NANCY: What about the dream theory of the non-Aryan people ?

SHARMA: Their dream theory led them to question the reality of the world. Is the world real, or just another dream ? Since existence is indeterminate, they shunned material possessions and advocated peace. They imagined God in the form of Shiva who shunned material possessions. Shiva means peace.

SHEKHAR: Do you think that's the reason they were so easily defeated by the early Aryan invaders ?

SHARMA: Maybe. But, you can't generalize. There must

have been exceptions. The battles between the Aryans and non-Aryans went on for several thousand years. During this period, the Aryans saw the beauty of the non-Aryan intellect. The Aryans wrote a new Veda in Sanskrit, the fourth Veda, compiling the knowledge and wisdom of the non-Aryans people. They called this Atharva Veda. This Veda includes a very short treatise called Maandukya Upanishad which is based on that dream theory. It questions: Is this world real, or is it just another dream ? Since the reality is indeterminate, they try to see an Absolute State which is beyond this variegated world, which is beyond the scope of human logic and reasoning, which is beyond the scope of human emotions and which is beyond all the measurements of Time and Space ...

NANCY: That sounds like the book "Tao of Physics".

SHARMA: Exactly. Here they try to see God as an abstraction of the Eternal Time and Space. The Sanskrit word for Time and Space is Kaala. Eternal Time and Space will be Mahaakaala. That's the perception of God of most of the tribal people in India. Mahaakaala is another name of Shiva.

SNEHA: Is Shiva a non-Aryan God !?

SHARMA: Originally, yes. There's no mention of Shiva in Rik, Yajur and Saama Veda. Shiva is mentioned only in Atharva Veda. Whereas the Aryans imagined their gods with jewels and ornaments, Shiva wore snakes for ornaments, displaying the unreality and futility of material possessions. The Aryans took several thousand years to understand and accept this idea.

NANCY: What about Kali, which is shown as the cruel, bloodthirsty, black and naked goddess in many movies ?

SHARMA: The word Kaala means Time. There is another meaning; it also means the black color. The black color denotes infinite space. When there is no color, it is black. That is the color of the outer space. Kali is the abstraction of the Eternal Time and Infinite Space. Any attempt to assign her a fashionable dress is asinine.

NANCY: Why do you allow them to disparage Kali in these Western movies ?

SHARMA: There are many mistakes and misgivings about India. See what happened to "Swastika", a Sanskrit word which actually means a symbol of peace for mankind ! That mistake has not yet been corrected ! Columbus voyaged to the West three times, and every time he thought North America was India and called the inhabitants "Indian", a mistake that has not been corrected in the last five hundred years. Correction about Kali will definitely take a little more time !

SHEKHAR: What about the propaganda of "lingam" as the phallic symbol ?

SHARMA: The same story ! Ignorance ! Whereas the migration of the Aryans into India can be dated between four to ten thousand years, the starting of the non-Aryans in India is buried in the abysmal past. Maybe two hundred thousand years ! The Dravidian folklore say that their land came from the depths of the ocean. Calculations do not fit to call it a geological continental drift, but the idea

270

is striking. The anthropological similarity and the philosophical similarity of Dravidians with the Australian aboriginal do indicate a deep past.

SHEKHAR: Maybe one hundred thousand years, contemporary to Cro-Magnon man of Europe !

SHARMA: Maybe. In that abysmal past, when the human brain was not yet ready for abstract thinking, man could imagine a connection with God only with something tangible, like an infinitely tall pillar rising into the sky. All over the world, ancient people tried to make tall towers --- stonehenges --- rising high into the sky. All the modern dictionaries admit that the origin of the word "lingam" is obscure. For the non-Aryans, "lingam" was an endless pillar which was their link with God.

NANCY: Link ? That sounds like a homonym !

SHARMA: Who knows where and how these words originated ! However, at the beginning, the Aryans used to laugh at everything said and done by the non-Aryans. The Aryans laughed at the "lingam" as a phallic symbol. They also laughed at Shiva, or Mahaakaala, the Supreme God of the non-Aryans, and gave out a lot of funny stories attributed to Shiva. After several thousand years, the Aryans accepted the non-Aryan ideas in a modified form. The great Atharva Veda emerged and Shiva became one of the Triumvirate of the Aryan Pantheon.

NANCY: That's interesting. You mean to say, although the Aryans were the conquerors, they finally accepted the non-Aryan teachings ?

SHARMA: Precisely. In fact, that was the starting point of Indian Civilization, where the Aryan aggressiveness was fused with the non-Aryan wisdom of understanding, acceptance and mutual respect.

SHEKHAR: How is it possible ? Aggressiveness is inconsistent with the concept of understanding, acceptance and mutual respect !

SHARMA: Aggressiveness is the "Agni", the Fire of the early Aryans. Fire burns everything down, but if controlled, it can be the starting point of civilization. Aggressiveness is necessary for survival, but it must be controlled by the norms of duty. That's Geeta, the famous book of Hinduism. It is a handbook of Duty ... a handbook that outlines how to conduct life, how to recognize duty at any particular post of life, how to sublimate the fire within us into peace and love.

NANCY: I still don't understand, if Indian Civilization is so great, how come they burn innocent brides for the dowry money ?

SHARMA: That happens ... let me repeat ... only in that part of India that was ruled by Islam for 664 years. The Indians who lived the abject life of a second class citizen for 664 years, lost all their former values of life and degenerated into a mindless, soulless crowd. They know nothing about Indian Civilization. Just because one is born near Delhi and carries a brown skin, he does not become an Indian. I have a name for them. In the absence of any other good name, I call them "Isthandu". Isthandus are the degenerated descendants of the time-servers who lost their national character during the 664 years of Islamic rule. Money is the top happiness for these people, because they don't understand any other happiness. They pose as high spiritualists, but in reality they are the lowliest materialists money can buy. All the degradations that you see in India today are due to one single cause --- the degeneration of these Isthandus who call themselves Indian.

NANCY: I'm amazed at your analysis. If the Isthandus are not Indian, how do you distinguish them from an Indian ?

SHARMA: There are a few tell-tale symptoms. As I explained earlier, the starting point of Indian civilization is based on "Shraddhaa", which means "Mutual Respect", between the Aryans and non-aryans. Today, that "mutual respect" is extended to include all the cultural groups that constitute India. Now, here is a litmus test: If you find a man who claims himself to be an Indian, but doesn't have respect for another culture in India, or claims superiority over another group or individual, he is not an Indian, he is an "Isthandu", he has inherited this from his Islamic masters, because Islam ruled India with the superiority complex of a conqueror. Islam never understood the tenets of "Shraddhaa", "Mutual Respect".

SHEKHAR: That's interesting ! Do you have any other symptom of these non-Indian "Indians" ?

SNEHA: I know one ! Those who burn girls in a dowry dispute ...

SHARMA: *(Interrupting)* ... or tolerate a dowry burning, they are definitely a miserable contradiction of everything

273

India stands for, they are not Indian, they are the Isthandus of the vilest order ...

NANCY: What about those who run for political gains by dividing people against people ...

SHARMA: They are Isthandu of the first category: lack of mutual respect. It is the same root cause, whether it's the burning of a bride in Delhi, or throwing of cow-heads in Amritsar, or inciting of tribals in Assam ...

Sharma did not know that after about a week, the teleprinter in the next room would be running wild with the news report that twenty thousand tribals came down from the hills to the plains of Assam with clubs and hatchets, ravaging everything on their way, killing five thousand men, women, children and babies in a single day with clubs, axes, knives and hatchets.

When the same news reached New Delhi, Phulraj called an urgent closed door meeting of senior party workers. There were high excitement and tension.

PHULRAJ: *(Reading a teleprinter message)* The tribals have killed five thousand Muslims at Nelli. The Parliament is convened. Do you have your speech ready ?

YASHPAL: Yes ! But, I can't blame the student leaders of Assam movement for this massacre !

Phulraj was very surprised.

PHULRAJ: Wha ... Why not ? That was the plan, wasn't it ?

YASHPAL: Yes. But, did you hear the foreign news ? The Assam leaders were in jail for the last twenty-five days. How can you blame them for ...

Phulraj was devastated when he heard that. "Who told you that ?" He could not recognize his own voice.

YASHPAL: Do you remember you allowed the foreign press to go to Assam ? Did you hear the BBC news ?

PHULRAJ: *(In extreme panic)* Oh my God, if we can't blame the Assam leaders, the Arab financiers will finish us for getting so many Muslims killed ! What shall I tell her now ? *(He tried to regain some self-control)* What about Farin ? That rascal is sitting there in Assam and didn't even tell me that he arrested the student leaders before ...*(picked up the telephone)* Shyam ?

Manmohan replied to the telephone.

MANMOHAN: *(To the telephone)* Shyam isn't here sir ! This is Manmohan.

PHULRAJ: *(To the telephone)* Where's Shyam ... *(Pause)* ... He has gone to watch the cricket match with West Indies ? You idiots ! Call up Assam and bring Farin to the phone.

YASHPAL: *(To Phulraj)* Does Mataji know anything about this ?

PHULRAJ: *(To the telephone, excitedly)* Farin, is that you ? You idiot, what are you doing sitting over there in Assam ...

Farin was contacted earlier by Shekhar about their trip to Assam. Luckily for Shekhar, Farin didn't know that there was breach between Shekhar and his father, Tyagi. Farin was more than happy to help the son of Mr. Tyagi ... the man known as the right hand man of the Prime Minister !

Although Farin was a senior IAS officer and a big boss to everybody else, he was like a wet cat to the private Secretary of the Prime Minister. Unfortunately, Nancy and Shekhar were sitting in his office at Gauhati in Assam when the telephone call came from Phulraj Mathur. Farin put his hand over the mouthpiece and told them ...

FARIN: *(To Nancy and Shekhar)* This is a trunk call from Prime Minister's office, New Delhi. Will you please ...

Nancy and Shekhar thanked him and walked out, closing the door behind them. Nancy and Shekhar talked outside in the porch.

NANCY: So, this is Assam ! It's much cooler here ! See those mountains and hills !

SHEKHAR: And those wild flowers !

NANCY: It is beautiful ! So, this was the shelter in history, "India-in-exile" for 664 years of Islamic rule ... the haven for those Indians who didn't want to live the life of a second class people in Islamic India ... !

SHEKHAR: According to Doctor Sharma.

NANCY: Do you have any other explanation ?

SHEKHAR: No. I'm starting to agree with his analysis !

NANCY: How soon can we go to see the tribal areas ?

SHEKHAR: You heard Mr. Farin ! If he gives us Police protection, we may go as early as tomorrow .... I hope he'll not find out what's going on between me and my father ...

However, inside his room, Farin was having a very rough time with Phulraj Mathur who was blasting him over the telephone, "Why did you arrest them without telling us ?"

Farin replied on the telephone, "That was as per

government policy ! "

Phulraj shouted on the telephone, "Government policy ? Are you trying to teach me government policy, you scum-head ? Why did you give that insulting remark about Assamese women ? You'll have to drink their urine in public, I'll see to it, you sewage-drinker !"

Manmohan, the Assistant to Phulraj, entered busily and gave a teleprinter message to Phulraj. Phulraj read it and told Farin over the telephone, "Do you know what you have done to us ? The Prime Minister went to the Parliament and, as per previous plan, gave a statement that the student leaders of Assam were responsible for the massacre at Nelli. And now I have a question here from the Embassy of Saudi Arabia, listen to this, you idiot, *(Phulraj read the teleprinter over the telephone)* "Since the student leaders were in jail for the last twenty-five days, how can the Prime Minister blame them for the massacre where five thousand Muslims were killed in a single day !"

As per another "previous" plan, the Golden Temple of the Sikhs at Amritsar was now surrounded by Indian Army. Artillery and machine guns were being lined up to shoot into the temple. The entire city of Amritsar was in great tension. Makkhanlal was sent to Amritsar to organize political groups to support army action.

But, three hundred miles away, back at Makkhan-lal's house in New Delhi, a different kind of unrest was building up.

TARA: What time Neel will come back ?

REENA: Neel won't be back today. He'll go directly to meet father at Amritsar.

TARA: On his way back from Amritsar, your father is supposed to see your father-in-law tomorrow. I'm glad

Neel will be there, too.

Reena asked ominously, "Why ? Do you want to do it today ?"

Tara nodded. Reena went to pour kerosene oil into a bucket from a container marked "KEROSENE: FLAMMABLE", while Tara was watching.

At the neighbor's house, there was a knock at the door. Mrs. Saxena looked up. She was working with Sona on a new doll. Mr. Saxena opened the door. Ashok was at the door, in Police uniform.

SAXENA: Are you coming to arrest me !

ASHOK: Yes, sir. I have a warrant for your arrest.

SAXENA: What's the charge ?

ASHOK: Sedition. Your report in Sharma's journal. I came to know that the Nepal Government has agreed to extradite Sharma, too.

SAXENA: You told me you'd give me time to dress up in my Military uniform !

ASHOK: Yes, of course. Please take your time.

At the neighbor's house, Neel's newly married wife, Laxmi, was seated on a sofa in the living room, reading a magazine. She had a lot of red vermillion at the parting of her hair. Vermillion is considered very auspicious by a Hindu woman. It is the sign of marriage ... sign of good health of the husband. Newly married girls, ... being new to vermillion, overdo it ... they put a lot on their hair !

Noticing that Laxmi was engrossed in reading the magazine, Tara signalled Reena to bring the bucket. Reena tiptoed to the back of the sofa with the bucket of kerosene oil in her hands. Unaware of the imminent danger, Laxmi was still engrossed in her magazine. She did not raise her head. She looked extremely beautiful in that angle, with a lot of red vermillion at the parting of her hair.

Tara was at the door of the living room getting ready with the matches. Reena suddenly unloaded the bucket of oil on Laxmi. Taken by surprise, Laxmi jumped out of the sofa and looked at Reena in utter disbelief. Instinctively, Laxmi turned towards the door, where Tara was standing, holding a lighted match, the flame flickering eerily. At the next instant, Tara threw the lighted match. Laxmi burst into flames.

Laxmi came running to the door, pushed Tara onto the ground, ran past her towards the backyard of Saxena's house. Her body was engulfed in flames, yet she ran, impelled by some super-human strength that people get just before death.

Saxena was in his living room, dressed in full military uniform, with medals shining, getting ready to get arrested and to be taken away to the prison. They all heard the screams of Laxmi and came out to the backyard. Laxmi, in flames, dropped in the backyard. Ashok tore off a window curtain and ran to her. He knelt down on the dirt and covered her body with the heavy curtain that extinguished the fire. Her voice was hardly audible ...

LAXMI: My sister-in-law threw the kerosene. My mother-in-law threw the match.

She collapsed.

Ashok didn't know that he could be so angry. He took charge of the situation and decided to do his duty to the fullest capacity of a Police Officer. He shouted for the policemen who were waiting in a van and in a jeep outside at the road.

ASHOK: *(Ordered to his assistant, pointing to Neel's house)* Go to that house. Arrest everybody. Put them in handcuffs and chains and throw them into the van. *(Ordered to another assistant)* Call the doctor. Get an ambulance.

The Police van left with Reena and Tara in handcuffs. Laxmi was taken into an ambulance van which was about to leave.

ASHOK: *(To Saxena)* You please take the jeep. I have to go to the hospital with the girl !

Ashok jumped into the ambulance. The ambulance left. Saxena got into the Police jeep and ordered the driver ...

SAXENA: Drive to the Golden Temple.

Golden Temple was in Amritsar, three hundred miles away ! The driver looked at him in surprise, not knowing what to do when an authoritative man in full military uniform gave a strange order.

SAXENA: Yes, Amritsar, straight to the Golden Temple. Another Mother is about to be burnt there. Let me see if I can stop that.

The jeep left. Sona threw her arms around the neck of Mrs. Saxena and cried inconsolably.

High up in Kathmandu, Sharma's office was raided by Nepalese Police, supervised by some Indian Police Officers. Sharma and Sneha, however, were hiding in a shed at the bottom of the hill.

SNEHA: I never thought that the Nepal Government would join hands with her so easily.

SHARMA: Everyone has their weaknesses. You must get ready to go back to India.

Sneha started to cry.

SNEHA: How can I leave you alone here !

SHARMA: Don't worry about me, Sneha ! I'll join the mountaineering team. They wanted me as their team doctor, anyway. You go back to India.

SNEHA: I can't leave you alone here !

SHARMA: Your Duty at this junction of life is in front of the Parliament Building in New Delhi. Go ! Organize the People. Take them with you and walk to the Parliament. Don't allow the Isthandus defile the Mother any more. India does not belong to the Isthandus ! Go ! Take charge of the Mother !

SNEHA: You please come with me. Your health is failing. You'll need medical care. Somebody will have to look after you !

Sneha cried and cried. She feared instinctively she would not see him again if she left him there.

SHARMA: Don't cry. I'll come back later, I promise. Right now, I've got to go to the mountains. The Himalayas had been the source of our strength since time immemorial. Throughout the ages, India has drawn her strength and wisdom from the high peaks of the Himalayas. India is in darkness today. I'll go to the high peaks. I'll bring back the light.

In the darkness of night, Sharma left for the Himalayas.

Shekhar and Nancy were at a distance of two thousand miles from Delhi ... in Assam ... waiting on a roadside, besides an overheated taxi. There was a range of low hills on one side of the road. The hood of the taxi was open and its radiator was steaming. The taxi driver tried to open the radiator cap, burnt his hand, licked it with a quick jerk, and told Shekhar ...

DRIVER: You'd better stay inside the taxi, please, sir ! This area is not good ! Tribals are out to take revenge !

NANCY: Revenge ? We've done no harm to them !

DRIVER: They don't know that !

SHEKHAR: Where's the Police escort Mr. Farin promised to send behind us !

NANCY: I think he's still talking to that angry women's delegation. Why does he gets into problems with women delegations almost all the time ?

SHEKHAR: He has a dirty sense of humor. Even a

287

rickshaw puller has better manners than he. The ladies don't like his remarks !

NANCY: And, he is, what-do-you-call-it, a senior IAS Officer ?

Shekhar and Nancy did not know that they were being watched by a group of tribal activists behind the bushes on the hills. Most of them had bows and arrows. Their leader had a gun. One of the bowman asked for permission, by signals, to strike with bow and arrows. The leader smiled and said, by signals, that he had something better than bows and arrows.

TRIBAL LEADER: *(Showing his rifle)* I want to use this gift I got from Indira Gandhi !! *(He laughed deliriously.)*

Shekhar saw a Police van at a distance ...

SHEKHAR: Oh, thank God, the Police escort has arrived at last !

NANCY: *(Looking in the same direction)* How do you know that's Police ?

At this time, there was a sudden burst of gunfire. The taxi got a number of bullet holes. The driver ducked

288

behind the car. Nancy shouted. Shekhar shouted in pain.

SHEKHAR: *(Shouted, holding his thigh)* They hit me !
They hit me !

The Police arrived. They jumped out of their van,
took position and started shooting towards the hill.

At the waiting room of the hospital in Gauhati,
the doctor was explaining to Farin and Tyagi.

DOCTOR: He is delirious with a very high fever.

TYAGI: *(To Farin)* You said in your telegram that his life
was not in danger !

DOCTOR: He got hit in the thigh. I thought that was not
dangerous. That's what I reported to Mr. Farin.

TYAGI: He'll be all right when he will see me. I've
something for him that'll perk him up. He rejected it in
the past, but I'm sure, he'll like it now !

Shekhar was in partial delirium in his hospital bed. Nancy was sitting at the bedside, holding his hand.

SHEKHAR: I'm the only one who knows all the pain. Do you know how much it hurts when you burn your hand ? Try it ! Try it ! Try it over your birthday candle. Try it over the candles on your coffin. Try it over the fire of your cremation. Try it ! Try it ! You'll know how much it hurts to burn your hand. They burnt my Kamla. Her whole body. Not just the hand. The entire body. Do you know how great her pain must have been ? I know. I know. I know.

Nancy looked up and saw Tyagi, Farin and the Doctor. Tyagi went to Shekhar and took his hand from Nancy. Nancy got up and walked away. The Doctor signalled Farin and Nancy to leave the room. They complied.

"Shekhar, Shekhar, my boy, see what I have here for you", Tyagi said. He had the Swiss Bank key in his palm. He thought Shekhar might have changed his mind.

In spite of his delirium, Shekhar recognized Tyagi and stared at him.

SHEKHAR: When did you come ?

TYAGI: Just one hour back.

SHEKHAR: Did Kamla come with you ?

Tyagi looked blankly at Shekhar.

TYAGI: It will be all right soon, Shekhar, I've collected everything for you that'll make you happy for the rest of your life.

Shekhar swelled into violent convulsions and ended up in a coma. The doctor tried to comfort him.

DOCTOR: This is going on again and again. Patients don't react like this just for a bullet wound in the thigh. It looks like some kind of poisoning. We don't have a toxicologist in our staff. I sent a telegram to Calcutta to send a toxicologist.

TYAGI: *(With ashen face)* Do you think it may be some kind of a poison ?

Doctor picked up a bullet from a plastic bag.

DOCTOR: This is the bullet we extracted from his thigh. Look, the bullet is very peculiar. It has a capillary hole. You should see it.

Doctor dropped the bullet in Tyagi's palm that had the ring with the large diamond shining on the other side of the finger. The key to the Swiss Bank account was shining on the palm. The bullet, with its capillary hole, dropped on the key and made a conclusive metallic sound.

292

Shekhar shouted again in his delirium.

SHEKHAR: Why did you not bring Kamla ? Kamla knows how much pain I am in ! Kamla should have come here to take me home ! My home ... somewhere ... in the clouds ... where she'll be waiting for me ... the flowers we had on our wedding night ... they'll bloom again ... and all the fragrance ...

DOCTOR: Mr. Tyagi, the patient is very upset at you. Let's go to the other room.

The Doctor escorted Tyagi out of the room and signalled Nancy to go in. Nancy sat at Shekhar's bedside and held his hand.

SHEKHAR: *(In delirium, exhausted)* She was so nice ! She gave love to everybody ! All the neighbors loved her. She was a real Laxmi. *(Looking at Nancy's eyes)* You know, my father told me he has everything for me to make me happy for the rest of my life. Life ! Life ! I'll be happy, really happy in my life. We'll go away, Kamla and myself ... far away ... we'll be drifting high above the clouds ... there's a beautiful flower garden there ... we'll play there ... we will run after the humming birds and drink the nectar from the flowers ... we will turn into humming birds ... we'll fly and balance like tiny helicopters ... Kamla will smile and blush like a new bride ... and we will drink ... we'll drink the nectar of life ...

Nancy did not say anything. Tears filled her eyes.

In front of the Golden Temple, guns were all lined up. Soldiers were aiming the guns towards the Temple. Saxena, in full Military uniform, arrived there on the jeep. He jumped out from the jeep, took position and gave orders to the soldiers ...

SAXENA: Stop it ! You can't shoot at that temple !

Soldiers were surprised. A few young soldiers wanted to confront Saxena, but an older soldier recognized him, and restrained the younger soldiers.

OLD SOLDIER: Wait a minute. He is the great Karak Bijli. Do you know, young guys, who is Karak Bijli ?

The Old Soldier stepped forward and saluted Saxena. Saxena took position facing the soldiers and guns. The Golden Temple was shining at his back. The Temple was reflected on the lake between him and the Golden Temple.

Saxena addressed his old artillery brigade in a full voice ...

SAXENA: My brothers from my old Artillery Brigade ! We have fought many battles together. We have fired those guns many times in our past. Every time we fired those guns, Mother India was behind us. Today, by mistake, you're aiming the guns at the Mother. Look at that Golden Dome ! The Golden Dome is shining like a golden locket over the heart of our Mother. If you shoot at that Dome, you will shoot through the heart of Mother India.

The CO (Commanding Officer) saw Saxena in his binoculars.

CO: Who's that man ?

A junior Army Officer arrived hastily to give him the news.

OFFICER: *(Panting)* He's Colonel Saxena, sir !

CO: He was kicked out of the Army ! What is he doing here ?

OFFICER: It his own Artillery Brigade, sir ! He's ordering the soldiers not to shoot at the Golden Temple.

CO: Cut him down ! We've orders from the Prime Minister ! Start shooting !

OFFICER: Sir, he's standing there facing the guns !

CO: Shoot through him ! We can't lose any more time.

The soldiers were waiting with loaded guns, aimed at the Golden Temple beyond the lake. Strangely enough, the water in the lake was very tranquil at that time. The reflection of the Golden Temple was shining in the lake. Saxena was standing facing the guns, on this side of the lake, appealing to the soldiers not to shoot. He was looking straight into the muzzles of the guns.

"Fire !"

The guns started to roar like thunders. When the thunder stopped, Saxena was not there any more. The Golden Temple was scarred with bullet holes.

The water of the lake was full of disturbances now. The reflection of the Temple was gone. The lifeless body of Saxena was rocking on water, creating more ripples, more disturbances.

When Nancy arrived Kathmandu and went to Sharma's log cabin, all that she saw were broken furniture and broken computers. Kancha, with one arm in a sling, came out limping and stared at her.

High up in the Himalayas, at their Base Camp Number 2, Sharma was attended by Willy, Jim and Bobby.

SHARMA: *(Jokingly)* I'm the official Medical Officer of the team, Jim ! You don't have to take care of me like that !

JIM: *(Jokingly)* I always wanted to give medicine to a doctor !

BOB: *(Impatiently)* Will you be OK today ? We must start our climb tomorrow !

Willy was looking down.

WILLY: Wait a minute ! Is that Nancy, by any chance, down at the Base Camp Number 1 ?

Willy grabbed a binocular and looked down at the camp below.

WILLY: That's Nancy ! That's Nancy !

BOB: Good Lord ! Now we'll be able to go back climbing, leaving Doctor Sharma with her !

JIM: Let's go down and bring her up !

Jim and Bob maneuvered downhill and reached Nancy and Kancha.

JIM: *(To Nancy)* Good Lord ! Where did you get these mountaineering clothes ?

NANCY: Kancha took me to a used clothing shop.

Nancy climbed up with the help of Jim and Bob. It was a difficult climb, but she managed it. Kancha stayed at the Base Camp Number 1.

Jim, Bob and Willy, aided by the Sherpas, were busy making arrangements to climb next day. Nancy and Sharma were catching up with the events. When Nancy told Sharma about Shekhar's death, he was silent for a long time.

SHARMA: Now he belongs to the Samudrarnava, the endless dance of particles, the Eternal Dance of Shiva beyond measurements of Time and Space ...

Nancy kept on looking at the ground, trying her best to hold her tears.

SHARMA: *(After a pause)* What will you do now ?

NANCY: I wanted to ask you the same question. I heard in Kathmandu that the Police will come here to get you.

SHARMA: They can't climb these mountains !

NANCY: What will you do if they climb here ?

SHARMA: They'll never reach me !

NANCY: Where is Sneha ?

Back in New Delhi, Sneha was leading a huge mass of demonstrators, mostly women, outside the Parliament Building. She was helped by Ashok and Shukla. The demonstrators marched in the roads, carrying the portrait of Laxmi. They shouted slogans like "Stop Dowry System" "Punish the Bride Burners" "Death to the Criminals", etc.

Inside the Parliament, Shukla was speaking to members who "represented" India.

SHUKLA: When we were young men, working as young volunteers for Mahatma Gandhi, we had a dream of building a free India that would have values higher than petty materialism. Gandhiji said that the Government Officers would not take any salary more than five hundred rupees per month. Everybody would work hard for the well being of the whole Nation. Money would not be considered as an indicator of social status. These goals were set according to the values and ideologies of Indian Philosophy. Gandhiji himself led a simple life and set an example to all of us.

Sometime in the year 1950, two years after the death of Mahatma Gandhi, a question was asked in this very Parliament. The question was directed to the then Prime Minister, Jawaharlal Nehru. The question was, "While the Government of India is promoting the Basic Education teachings of Mahatma Gandhi, why are you sending your own grandsons, Rajeev and Sanjeev, to expensive English medium schools ?" The answer was interesting. Nehru replied, "Those people who can afford will definitely send their children to better schools."

Mahatma Gandhi's ideology of simple living was crushed. New standards were set up by Nehru himself. "People who can afford". Everyone tried his best to qualify as "the people who can afford" in a country that preached supremacy of human soul over amassing material possessions. Nehru himself admitted in his book, "The Discovery of India", that he never understood the philosophy of "Adwaita". He led the country as its Prime Minister for the first seventeen years of independence.

Today, after about thirty-five years of independence, we find that we've turned into the most despicable materialists that money can buy. All values of human life have evaporated. A bride is burnt for a refrigerator. A bride is burnt for a television. A bride is burnt for a VCR. A bride is burnt for a few thousand rupees. Five hundred girls are burnt every year near Delhi alone ! Just for a refrigerator, a television, a VCR, or a bicycle ! And nobody complains ! Nobody minds ! Everybody accepts it as a matter of fact. If anybody complains, he is accused of giving a bad name to the country and is dubbed as unpatriotic.

The root cause of this inextricable social evil is embedded deep in our national character. As I'm getting older, I can see that all the maladies of India today ... like the poisoning of Assam in the East or bombarding of the Golden Temple in the West ... just for some short-sighted political gains, similar to money gains in a dowry deal, ... all these come from the same root, the loss of the Soul of the Nation. Somewhere deep in the history, we lost a very valuable possession, the Soul of the Nation. We have become a soulless people. I beg my countrymen to go and find it. We will not survive as a human society if we lose our soul.

The demonstrators outside are claiming justice for the death of one girl. Her name was Laxmi. Thousands of girls are killed every year. Each one of them is the Laxmi of the country. Let me repeat. Each one of them is the Laxmi of the country. We want justice for each one of the case. The criminals of each case must be brought to justice. But, the greatest criminals are those who cover up these cases, who condone these crimes, who ignore these ghastly incidents. All of them must be brought to justice. By burning these girls, you have burnt the Laxmi of the country. By poisoning the golden rice-fields of Assam, by firing machine guns at the Golden Temple, you have pierced a bullet through the heart of Mother India."

The demonstrators outside went on marching. They shouted slogans: "Stop Dowry System" "Punish the Bride Burners" "Death to the Criminals", etc.

Sneha was tired and stopped for a drink of water. She was joined by Ashok who was in plain clothes.

ASHOK: I'll start the journal of Doctor Sharma again.

SNEHA: *(Enthusiastically)* I'll be always on your side ... *(continued, with some doubt)* if you want me to be ...

ASHOK: I'll always work with you, if you agree ...

There was something very special in Ashok's voice. It touched a vulnerable chord inside of Sneha. She blurted, very much incoherently, "I'm so ugly !"

Ashok's reply was full of affection and understanding, "No ! You're the most beautiful girl I've ever seen in my entire life !"

The demonstrators went on and on around the Parliament Building, shouting the slogans.

From a ledge not too far below Base Camp Number 3 in the Himalayas, Sharma and Nancy looked down to the Base Camp Number 2, more than a thousand feet below. Camp Number 2 appeared to be very small when seen from this vantage point. The tents, colored red, dark green and black, to be discernible against an icy, white background, appeared like small rectangles of the size of playing cards. The Police Officials who occupied the Camp appeared like a handful of small, moving dots.

NANCY: I wish I could inform Jim or Willy to come down and help you !

SHARMA: No, I can manage it ! I wanted to climb these mountains all my life !

Nancy looked up when she heard Jim's cry from above.

JIM: Why are you climbing without a rope ?

NANCY: *(Shouted)* Can you throw some ropes ?

Jim and Willy climbed down, with ropes, and with all the maneuvers known in their mountaineering expertise. These were very difficult mountains. The climbing back was much more strenuous. With great efforts, they took Sharma and Nancy up to the upper Base Camp Number 3.

JIM: We've got to go up. Bob is waiting half way up.

SHARMA: I'll go with you.

WILLY: *(To Sharma)* I think you should take a rest here. Nancy will look after you.

JIM: The wind is very unpredictable at this altitude, Nancy ! You must be very careful.

NANCY: What do you mean ?

WILLY: We lost quite a few tents over here !

NANCY: Blown away by the wind ?

JIM: Yes. You'll never know when the wind will turn into a strong gust.

Jim and Willy climbed up, attended by Sherpas.

NANCY: *(To Sharma)* Would you like to go into the tent and get some rest ?

Sharma stood up and looked at the magnificent Himalayas. Snow peaks. The sky was intense blue.

SHARMA: Look at the peak, Nancy ! So magnificent ! It always reminds me of ancient India. The Philosophy that we reached was a zenith of the human mind. At that summit, our experience of a variegated world vanishes into a point. Even the difference between an individual soul and God cannot be discerned at that vanishing point. That is Adwaita, where everything is seen as a manifestation of Brahman.

NANCY: You mean God ?

SHARMA: The word Brahman cannot be translated as God. The Western world has an idea about a fixed God who created the universe. In Hinduism, there is no difference between the Creator and the Creation. That's why Hinduism cannot be called a religion. It is only a way of life.

NANCY: What about Adwaita ? Is it another religion ?

SHARMA: No. Adwaita is not a religion. It is ... just ... wisdom. Look ! Look at that red colored tent !

NANCY: *(With some surprise)* What about the red colored tent ?

SHARMA: There is a piece of sky inside that tent. In the wisdom of Adwaita, there is no difference between the Creator and the Creation, like there is no difference between the infinite, blue sky and the sky within that red colored tent ! In the wisdom of Adwaita, all human beings appear as Children of Immortal Bliss, as kith and kin imbued in universal love. I want to climb to that summit. I want to take my countrymen back to that peak. Once they reach that peak, all the desires for material possessions, all the desires for petty glorifications, all the desires for conflicting needs will vanish into Akaal, Timelessness. The World will become peaceful and the ocean of non-possessive, universal love will fill everybody's heart.

NANCY: Where are you going ?

SHARMA: I'm going to climb that peak.

A dense fog was rising in the gorge behind Sharma. He appeared unreal, partially silhouetted against the white fog.

NANCY: You can't climb without a rope !

SHARMA: Let me climb this mountain without a rope.

In spite of all the protests from Nancy, Sharma started to climb the mountain only with an ice axe. Watching him from below, Nancy became scared and nervous. Very soon, the rising fog covered everything.

As predicted by Jim and Willy, the wind started to blow harder and harder without any warning. Its fury would subside for a while, then bluster with a piercing sound at the next moment.

After some time, a strong gust of wind blew off the red tent.

When Nancy came climbing down, aided by a Sherpa, to the Base Camp Number 2, the Police were gone. She then climbed down to the Base Camp Number 1. Police were gone from there, too. The Sherpa who helped Nancy said goodbye and climbed back to the upper camps. Nancy was expecting Kancha at that Base Camp. She went to the front of a tent and called ...

NANCY: Kancha, are you there ?

Neel came out from the tent. Nancy was taken aback.

NANCY: Neel ?

NEEL: I've been waiting here for you, Nancy ! I asked the Police party to wait for me, but they wouldn't ! It's so scary to wait over here all by myself !

NANCY: What do you want ?

NEEL: I've come to meet Jim and Willy also.

NANCY: Why ?

NEEL: I want to apologize to them. I want to apologize to you ! I want to apologize to everybody !

NANCY: You don't have to apologize to anybody ! Just go away ! That's all !

NEEL: No. I must talk to Jim. He was such a good friend ! I became angry at Shekhar and sent those calculations to the Royal Geographic Society ...

NANCY: *(Surprised)* You did what ?

NEEL: I was thinking Shekhar encouraged you to disrupt my wedding ...

Nancy became very concerned.

NANCY: What happened with the Royal Geographic Society ? Are they coming here ?

NEEL: No. They wrote me back that the observations in that field book were wrong. Every winter snow builds up on this peak, making a vertical column of ice that rises very high. In summer, that vanishes.

NANCY: So ?

NEEL: I have to apologize to everybody. It's not the highest peak.

NANCY: It's still the highest peak, Neel ! Only you don't

know how to see it !

NEEL: I have to apologize to you. I doubted you for no reason. You didn't disturb my wedding.

NANCY: What happened to your wedding ?

NEEL: My mother and sister are in jail. They burnt Laxmi to death.

    Nancy gasped.

NANCY: Oh my God !

NEEL: My father is in jail, too ! All his alleged connections with Indira Gandhi ... nothing could save him. I'm all by myself now. I don't have anybody to talk to. Will you forgive me ? Will you allow me to be your friend again ? Let's go back to MIT ! We'll have our old life back .... I promise I'll never betray you again. You should understand ... how my family put pressure on me. This will never happen again, I promise, I ... *(fearfully)* What's that ?

    Nancy took out her pistol. Neel saw it and became very frightened.

NEEL: No ! No ! No ! You're not going to shoot me, are you ? Nancy, Nancy, don't shoot ...

    Neel ran backwards till he reached the edge of the precipice. He could not go any further back.

NANCY: Don't go too far, Neel ! Not more than thirty-five feet. This gun will stop a pig at thirty-five feet, they told me. You are not a pig ! You're a real brain ! Nobody will like that brain to be spilled four hundred feet below ... down that cliff.

NEEL: Nancy, don't shoot, don't forget how much you loved me at one time ...

NANCY: *(Laughed)* Love ??? Are you still using that word ?

NEEL: Nancy, Nancy, please, let me live, I will never bother you again ... I'll never come to see you again ...

NANCY: You want to cling to life, no matter what, ha ! What about Laxmi ? She was a young girl who wanted to live, too !

NEEL: Don't blame me for something that was done by my mother and sister. I never told them to burn ...

NANCY: But you do know that dowry leads to burning of the bride. You do know that thousands of girls are burnt every year. You don't care for their lives. You care only for your own life ! I want to teach you how it feels when you lose your life. Let me take off the silencer so that you hear the sound.

Nancy fired. With a blasting sound that reverberated in the surrounding mountains, the bullet hit dust some three feet on Neel's left. Neel jumped and fell on ground.

NEEL: Nancy, Nancy, don't, don't ...

Nancy fired again. This time the bullet hit dust some three feet on Neel's right. Neel rolled on ground, cried begging for his life.

NEEL: Nancy, Nancy, please, please, I beg you, I beg you, ...

NANCY: Don't think my aim is bad. I practiced with this gun many times. I could shoot right through your eye. You just tell me which eye you want to give, right or left ...

NEEL: Nancy, Nancy, please, please, I beg you, I beg you, ...

NANCY: All right. Get up. Now you know the value of life. Go back and tell them who don't understand the value of life. *(Yelled at the top of her voice)* Go, get up, run, don't show me your face again !

Neel got up, turned, ran to the right, and then he ran downhill. Nancy watched him running downhill, falling many times, and vanishing behind a bend. Nancy was still holding the gun. Then, suddenly, she threw the gun that made a long trajectory to a small stream some five hundred feet below. Nancy fell to her knees and started to cry.

When the mountaineering team came back to the Base Camp Number 1, there was a lot of activities. More tents. The Sherpas were busy packing up, supervised by Bob and Willy. Jim was talking to Nancy at one side.

NANCY: But, I told you what Neel told me ...

JIM: Forget Neel ! Nobody has seen it. Due to some unexplained atmospheric turbulence, snow and ice builds up vertically. The top of that huge ice column will still be the highest spot on the earth. Don't release any publicity now. We'll be back in winter, deep winter. That's when the snow build-up will be at the maximum.

NANCY: What happened to Doctor Sharma ?

JIM: I saw him going up and up. I asked him to wait for us and take the rope, he refused. The sky was very blue. He said ... that vertical column of ice will show him the way to the infinity. I did not see him fall. Bob saw it from the other side. If Bob is right, his body fell some six thousand feet. I did not see it, though. All that I saw ---

he was going up and up and up.

NANCY: He said he would go and bring back something.

JIM: What will you do now ?

NANCY: Me ?

JIM: Yes. You should come back with us to the States.

NANCY: No. Not now. I have some plans of my own.

The mountaineering team went back to the United States after a week or two. Nancy did not go with them. She went straight to Mother Ayesha's Convent, looking for Apu. Apu had a high fever at that time. He was very restless, fidgeting from side to side.

AYESHA: Since you'd left, he had at least four or five spells of this fever.

Nancy held the hot body of the child firmly to her bosom. Gradually, Apu became calm and restful, like a river that has finally arrived at the ocean. After some time, he fell asleep in Nancy's arms.

"Has his speech improved ?", Nancy asked.

"Just the same word", Mother Ayesha replied, "the only word, Nehi."

"Meaning "Don't", isn't it ?"

"That too only when he is excited. Otherwise he won't talk, as if his lips are sealed. He would be drawing pictures only ... pictures of a woman in a sari ... and then smear it with red crayons. I saved all his pictures. A psychologist may want to see these, if and when we can afford one."

Nancy laid Apu on the bed and covered him with a blanket. Apu slept snugly. Nancy checked the heap of Apu's drawings. She found some sketches other than the woman in a sari. It was a woman in a green skirt and a yellow blouse ... smeared with red crayons. She showed it to Mother Ayesha.

"That must be you !", Mother Ayesha said, "Somehow, you have entered his mind. Maybe he sees his mother in you !"

Mother Ayesha left Apu with Nancy and went to her office. Nancy looked at the sketches for a long time. That evening, she went to see Mother Ayesha at her office.

"Mother, can I stay here and work for you as a volunteer ... and, look after Apu ... and other children and ... "

"Of course you can", Mother Ayesha reassured Nancy, "we'll be more than happy to have you here." Then, she added hesitantly, "But, you know that we have very little to offer to you, all the works are voluntary, there is no salary ... "

"I know that", Nancy interrupted, "you don't have to give me any salary. On the other hand, I'll go and raise funds for you in the United States, I know a lot of people who will like to donate ... "

After a few days, Ashok and Sneha came to see Nancy at the Convent and they talked for a long time. Ashok had resigned his job as an IPS officer. Both Ashok and Sneha were running the news paper, in spite of all the hurdles. The three of them went on meeting frequently. Nancy raised money and bought a few computers for the news paper. She also collected donations for Mother Ayesha's convent for burn victims.

After about a month, there came an overseas telephone call for Nancy. Nancy went to Ayesha's office to take the call.

NANCY: *(To the telephone)* Yes, Uncle Vinny, let him go ! I'll stay here and work for Mother Ayesha for a while. I'll keep you posted … *(Pause)* … No, I don't want to go back now. How much money you said you wanted to spend in my wedding ? … *(Pause)* … What did you say ? One hundred and fifty thousand dollars ?? OK, Uncle Vinny, send the money down here. I'll give it to Mother Ayesha's convent for burn victims… *(Pause)* No, I don't have to marry … I've already got a son … a five year old son … he's so cute, you won't believe … *(Pause)*… As I told you, I'll work for Mother Ayesha for some time, and then I'll decide. I love this work, you know that ! *(Pause)* Yes, Uncle Vinny, there was a time when I was always worried only about my own problems, my own pain. Now, I don't care for my own pain at all. There are so much of pain all over, my own pain doesn't look important any more. *(Pause)* Yes, let him go … I'll call you again.

THE END